CHRISTMAS THREAT

HAZARDOUS HOLIDAY

LYNN SHANNON

CHRISTMAS THREAT

Copyright © 2022 by Lynn Balabanos

Published by Creative Thoughts, LLC

All rights reserved.

No part of this book may be reproduced in any form or by any electronic or mechanical means, including information storage and retrieval systems, without written permission from the author, except for the use of brief quotations in a book review.

This book is a work of fiction. Names, characters, businesses, organizations, places, events and incidents either are the product of the author's imagination or are used factitiously. Any resemblance to actual persons, living or dead, events, or locales is entirely coincidental.

Cover design by Maria Spada.

Scripture appearing in this novel in whole or in part from THE HOLY BIBLE, NEW INTERNATIONAL VERSION®, NIV® Copyright © 1973, 1978, 1984, 2011 by Biblica, Inc.™ Used by permission. All rights reserved worldwide.

Peace I leave with you; my peace I give you. I do not give to you as the world gives. Do not let your hearts be troubled and do not be afraid.

John 14:27

ONE

The boot prints weren't supposed to be there.

Faith Hicks gripped the handle of the feed scoop. Chickens gathered at her feet, clucking happily as they ate the grains scattered on the ground. They were free-roaming hens, but last night's thunderstorm and icy temperatures had driven them to take shelter in the coop. Two boot prints were encased in the mud surrounding the structure. Large. Man-sized.

A chill rippled down Faith's spine as she glanced over her shoulder. The two-bedroom ranch house stood silent behind her. Christmas lights dangled from the eave and a Santa waved from the kitchen window. The barn, a short distance away, was closed up tight. A giant wreath hung above the main door. Water still clung to the fake greenery, ice crystals sparkling in the morning sunshine. Everything was as it should be.

Except for those boot prints. Who had been on her property?

Faith didn't have any close neighbors. She'd inherited

the farm from her grandparents, and it was over ten acres, most of it wooded. It bothered her to think of someone being so close to her house. Cutler, Texas was a small town, but bad things happened everywhere. She'd watched enough real-life crime shows to know that much.

Whoever left the boot prints had been wandering around in the early-morning hours, otherwise the rain would've washed the evidence away. Faith stepped closer and noticed another set of prints. These were smaller, made by a woman or a teenager. The strides were also longer, the threads similar to tennis shoes, pressed firmly in the mud. Had the person been running? Maybe.

How strange. Faith couldn't make heads or tails of it, and indecision warred within her. Chase, her childhood friend, was an officer with the Cutler Police Department. Should she call and tell him about the impressions? Probably. Her cell phone was in the house. She'd finish her chores, take some photos, and send them to him.

Chances were, it was nothing. Her closest neighbors—the Bradleys—had a teenage daughter and a disobedient puppy. Maybe their dog had drifted too far from home this morning and they'd come onto the property to collect him. Yes, that must be it. Their daughter had chased after the puppy in a hurry and was followed by her dad.

Except...there were no puppy prints. Faith glanced over her shoulder again, her gaze skipping over the buildings. All seemed well.

Still, better to mention it to Chase anyway. Just in case. Faith had a security alarm in her house and a front-door camera. Safety wasn't something she thought about often, but she was wise enough to recognize the risks of being a woman on her own in a rural area.

She didn't even have a decent guard dog. Scamper was pushing old age and rarely barked. The golden Lab-mix was more likely to lick an intruder to death than bite him. As if to prove her point, he rolled in the grass nearby and sighed with contentment as the sunshine warmed his fur. Faith laughed. "Life is good, huh, Scamp?"

He barely opened his eyes. The chickens circled around him, and Scamper paid them no mind either. He'd been Faith's constant companion since she adopted him from the shelter last year. Mellow, easy-going, and loving, Scamper had been a balm to her broken heart. She adored him.

Wintery wind rustled her ponytail, a reminder that Christmas was only a week away. A pang of sorrow washed over Faith. Her second holiday season as a widow. This was not the life she'd envisioned for herself at thirty. Family, a loving husband, and a house full of kids had always been her dream. Losing Mitch suddenly to an aneurysm had put her on a new course. A solitary one.

She had family. Her parents were warm and caring, her extended relatives a mere phone call away. She had friends who would come running if needed. But it wasn't the same. As time worn the edges off her initial grief, the loneliness crept in, taking over quiet moments of her day. She and Mitch had been married only six months when he died. They'd barely settled into their new life together before it was ripped away.

Shaking off her morose thoughts, Faith returned the feed scoop to the shed and shut the door. A quick glance at her watch confirmed she needed to hurry or she'd be late for work. Her daycare, First Steps, was the only one in town. Faith was proud of the business she'd built from the ground up, but it took a lot of energy. Thankfully, she had ten full-time employees, including an office manager to help.

She headed for the barn. The scents of hay and horse wafted out when Faith opened the main door. Poppy swung her head over the stall door and nickered in greeting. She was brown with a white flame down the center of her nose. Mitch had bought her for Faith as a wedding present. He'd loved animals as much as she did.

Faith rubbed the horse's nose. "Morning, girl."

A cold chill rustled the strands of her hair, brushing them against her left cheek. She froze. Something wasn't right…The wind was coming from the back of the barn, but that door should be closed. Faith had latched it herself to protect Poppy against the wind drummed up by the thunderstorm.

Faith abandoned the horse and moved farther into the barn. Sure enough, the rear door—big enough for a person to walk through—was open. The image of the boot prints flashed in her mind's eye. Instinct had Faith reaching for the pitchfork leaning against the wall. Had someone been in her barn? Were they still there?

Mentally, she berated herself for leaving her cell phone in the house. But what was she going to do? Call the police and tell them someone might or might not be in her barn? Her heart pounded as scenarios from the shows she'd watched flashed through her brain. Faith mentally gave herself a shake. She was being ridiculous. Scaring herself wasn't the answer.

Chase. She could call Chase and have him come and

take a look. What was the use of having a guy as your best friend if you couldn't occasionally ask him to kill spiders or inspect your barn for an intruder? He'd come, find nothing, and they'd have a good laugh about it. Faith would have to endure the teasing for months, but it was a small price to pay. Deep down, she knew he'd be furious if she didn't call.

Faith tightened her grip on the pitchfork and edged backward toward the open door. She took a deep breath to calm her racing heart, straining to hear any noise out of the ordinary.

A mewing sound came from the tack room.

Her steps faltered. What on earth? It sounded like a kitten.

The cry came again, louder this time. Faith's heart stuttered as recognition sank into her from years of working with children. Her own safety forgotten, she raced for the tack room, swinging the door open wide.

The room was a mess. Saddles had been toppled from their resting place. Bridles, normally hung on the wall, were scattered across the concrete floor. The wail grew in strength. Faith followed the sound to the corner of the room, her eyes not quite believing what her mind already knew was true.

A baby. A little girl, judging from the pink blanket wrapped around its small form and the matching knitted hat on her head. She was nestled in a pile of horse blankets. Her sweet face was turning pink from crying, tears leaking from her eyes to run down plump cheeks.

Shock rippled through Faith. She had dozens of questions, but the infant wasn't going to answer them. Priorities first. Get the baby to the house and call the police.

Faith was halfway across the room, bent on scooping up the little girl, when the scuffle of a shoe against concrete came from behind her. She whirled. A man stood in the doorway, dressed in black, with a ski mask over his face. He held a lead rope for a horse in his hands. Stretched out. As if...with a sudden clarity and focus, Faith knew he meant her harm.

He intended to strangle her.

Faith screamed, raising the pitchfork still clasped in her hand. She jabbed forward. The intruder leapt back, but she didn't give him a moment to recover. She kept charging. She wouldn't allow him to hurt her, or the precious baby in her tack room. Someone was yelling like a mad woman and Faith didn't realize until much later that it was her.

He attempted to grab the pitchfork with a gloved hand. Faith dodged. She couldn't allow him to get close to her, since his strength would easily overpower her. The intruder sidestepped. The move threw Faith off balance. She stumbled and nearly fell.

The opening was all he needed.

He grabbed the pitchfork. For a terrifying heartbeat, they wrestled for control over the makeshift weapon. Then a flash of inspiration had Faith loosening her grip. The masked man felt it, and his muscles relaxed for just a second. Hatred and evil poured off him. The lead rope was still clutched in his hand.

God, please. Let this work.

Blood pulsing in her ears, Faith lunged suddenly. Her attacker stumbled back against the horse stall. His scream ricocheted around the barn as the pitchfork impaled his thigh.

Faith dropped her end and spun toward the tack room. In moments, she had the baby in her arms. She didn't dare spare a glance at the man writhing on the barn floor in pain. Her entire focus was getting away from him. Clutching the infant to her chest, she raced from the barn as though the devil himself were on her heels.

Her feet pounded against the grass. The world narrowed to her farm house, the back door signaling safety. Faith urged her body to move faster. Her instincts screamed that the intruder might not be alone. There could be more. She had no idea what was going on.

She bolted onto the porch. Her fingers trembled as she twisted the knob on her back door. It swung open, and she darted inside, slammed the door behind her, and then twisted the locks into place. Chest heaving, she backed away. Her gaze went to the large picture window overlooking the yard. Scanning, searching for any sign of the intruder heading her way. The baby in her arms stirred.

Her phone. She needed to call the police—

She rammed into something solid. Rough hands landed on her shoulders.

Faith screamed.

TWO

Chase McKenzie grunted as Faith's elbow landed in his rib cage. He immediately released her shoulders, her terrified scream shocking in its intensity. She spun to face him. Chase held up his hands in the classic sign of surrender. "It's just me. I'm sorry, I didn't mean..."

His gaze swept over her, his mind registering several things at the same time. Faith's gorgeous honey-colored eyes were wide with fear. Strands of sable hair had floated free of her askew ponytail, her breathing was ragged as if she'd run a thousand miles, and clutched to her chest was a bundle that suspiciously looked like a baby. The tiny creature wailed as if to answer Chase's silent question before he'd asked it.

Yet. Definitely a baby.

Something was very wrong. Faith was unflappable. Levelheaded, intelligent, and kindhearted. As the owner of a daycare, she spent her days comforting babies and wrangling toddlers with grace and skill. The very thought of handling one kid was enough to have Chase shaking in his boots, let alone dozens. He'd never seen Faith breathless and afraid. And where on earth did she get a baby from?

"What happened?" His attention shot to the area behind Faith. The kitchen was empty. Still, his hand automatically reached for the weapon normally holstered on his hip. His fingers only found the fabric of his worn blue jeans. He was on vacation. Chase was an officer with the Cutler Police Department, but a friend from college was getting married over the weekend and he'd requested time off to attend.

Faith sucked in a breath and rocked the infant. Her gaze fixed on the picture window overlooking the backyard. "I found this baby in the tack room. I don't know where she came from, but then a man appeared and he attacked me. I escaped and ran to the house."

A familiar dose of rage pumped through Chase's veins. Faith sparked his protective instincts. Always had. They'd been close for as long as he could remember. Their mothers were best friends, which made Faith a part of his childhood —a part of him—in an indescribable way. She was like his left arm or the air in his lungs. Vital. Chase wouldn't let anyone hurt her. Ever.

What Chase wouldn't allow himself to think about was the deeper meaning of his feelings for Faith. They were friends. That's all they would ever be. Chase had never been—and would never be—good enough for her. They both knew it. Faith cared deeply about him, that much was certain, but she'd never once looked at him with any romantic interest.

His gaze swept over her again. "Are you injured?"

She shook her head. "No."

"Is the man who attacked you still in the barn?" His tone was sharp, the question coming out clipped.

If Faith was bothered by it, it didn't show in her expression. Her gaze stayed locked on the backyard. "I don't know. I stabbed him with the sharp end of my pitchfork, so it's possible." She winced. "He screamed."

Chase felt no sympathy for the intruder. Faith had every right to defend herself by whatever means necessary. Imagining how terrifying the encounter must've been for her heated his blood. And what about the baby? Where had she come from?

A thousand more questions ran through his mind, but Chase held his tongue. There would be time for explanations later. Right now, he needed to arrest Faith's attacker.

Chase bent over and removed his backup weapon from the holster on his ankle. He didn't carry his service weapon while off duty, but he was never unarmed. "Call the police, Faith, and lock the door behind me."

She clutched his arm. "Shouldn't you wait for backup?"

He should, but Faith lived a good twenty minutes from the police station. The intruder in her barn could be long gone before they arrive. A man willing to attack a woman on her own property needed to be behind bars for the safety of the entire town.

Chase briefly touched her fingers before shaking off her hold. "Lock the door, Faith."

Without another word, he slipped out of the house onto the porch. Scamper greeted him with a nose bump. Normally, he would stop to rub the old dog's ears, but Chase didn't have the luxury now. He also didn't want the Lab getting hurt. "Stay, Scamp."

Chickens scattered as Chase ran across the yard toward the barn. Sunshine warmed his shoulders, but wintery bluster and thunderclouds forming in the distance promised more rain. More cold. Forecasters were predicting snow for Christmas.

The barn doors were open, but no one was visible. Chase gripped his gun with both hands. He used the side of the barn for cover, listening for any sounds emanating from inside.

Nothing.

He swung around the corner, weapon raised. His gaze swept the interior of the barn in quick snaps. A pitchfork lay on the ground in front of Poppy's stall and a dark red stain dotted the concrete. A trail of blood led to the opposite door of the barn. Chase followed it, careful to keep his senses on alert, but his instincts said the intruder had escaped.

His conclusion was confirmed when he reached the other side of the barn. Tamped-down grass and broken branches indicated someone had plowed through the bushes at the edge of the woods. There was a farm road on the other side of the trees. It was likely the attacker had escaped in his car. Chase wanted to look for tire tracks, but he'd wait for the other officers to arrive. He didn't want to leave Faith and the baby alone.

He returned to the interior of the barn. Poppy hung her head over the stall door, and he stroked her nose before crouching to examine the pitchfork. Two of the prongs had blood on them, but only at the edges. The attacker was hurt, but not badly enough to prevent him from getting away. He might need a doctor though. Stitches.

Chase jogged back to the house and knocked on the door.

Faith appeared, the baby in her arms, relief flashing across her beautiful face. She unlocked the door and opened it. "The police are on their way. He got away?"

"Afraid so." He holstered his weapon. "Explain to me exactly what happened."

Faith ran through the chain of events, starting with the boot prints and ending with the assault in the barn. Every word from her mouth made Chase's concern grow. He assessed the scattered objects in the tack room, his stomach sinking. Then he rejoined her where she waited outside the barn.

Faith patted the infant's back with her left hand. The faint tan line where her wedding ring used to be still lingered. "What do you think?"

He wanted to shield her from the horrible theories forming in his brain, but that wouldn't do either of them any good. Especially since Chase feared the danger was far from over. Still, he could start with the good news.

"I think you're a brave woman." His mouth twitched. "I also believe your intruder is in serious pain after finding himself at the wrong end of your pitchfork. Smart move, Faith. If I'd known how dangerous you were, I wouldn't have used my key to come into the house."

That earned him a faint smile. "I always look before turning my pitchfork on someone."

He rubbed his rib cage. "You didn't when you jabbed me with your elbow. That bony thing should be classified as a weapon all on its own."

She laughed, as he'd hoped, and attempted to slug his

arm. He caught her wrist and pulled her close for a hug, careful not to disturb the sleeping baby nestled against her. The truth of what could've happened to Faith sank into Chase with sharp claws. She could've died. The thought stole his breath. "I'm glad you're okay."

She sighed, leaning against him. "What aren't you telling me, Chase?"

No one understood him like Faith did. Growing up, he'd been something of a rebel. He'd fooled his mother, charmed his teachers, and wiggled out of more trouble than he'd care to remember. But the one person who always saw right past all his defenses was Faith. She demanded authenticity from him.

It's what made their friendship so hard to navigate. Chase was terrified that one day she'd realize the truth about his feelings toward her. And once that happened… there was no going back. It would change their friendship forever. It wasn't worth the risk.

Sirens wailed in the distance. His colleagues were on their way.

Faith pulled back to look him in the face. Her mouth was set in a determined line. Sunlight caressed the curve of her cheek and the sweep of her jaw. Her porcelain skin was smooth save for the freckle under her left eye and the faint scar above her lip from when she fallen at the roller rink when they were twelve. The woman was stunning. Chase kept thinking that one day he'd become immune to her beauty, but it never happened.

She arched one brow, meeting his gaze straight on. "Tell me."

Sugarcoating wouldn't work. Not with Faith. Better to rip the bandage off all at once.

"Whoever your attacker was, he chased someone into your barn." Chase jutted his chin toward the baby. "Probably her mama. He assaulted her, maybe killed her. Then he carried her body from the barn...to somewhere. The woods, perhaps, or to his vehicle parked on the road. And then he came back for the child."

Faith paled as her hand cradled the baby's head in a protective gesture. "But I was here."

Chase nodded. He didn't have to say the rest. It was obvious in the way her eyes darkened, Faith had figured it out. Her barn was a potential murder scene. If he was right, and the baby's mom was dead, then Faith was a witness.

Judging from the way the criminal had come after her in the barn...

He intended to silence her. For good.

THREE

Hours after the attack, Faith's hands still trembled.

Rain pattered against the kitchen window as police officers bustled between the barn and woods. Crime scene tape bounced in the wind. The stark black and yellow colors were a sharp contrast to the cheery Christmas decorations in the house. This morning's events felt like a bad dream, but the child in her arms and the chaos in her yard proved it'd been real.

The back door opened, and moments later, Chase stepped inside the kitchen. His thick black hair was damp from the rain. Although it wasn't even noon yet, a dusky shadow darkened his strong jaw, drawing attention to the deep cleft in his chin. He had shed his jacket in the mudroom. A flannel shirt encased his broad shoulders and was tucked into worn blue jeans. She'd given the button-down to Chase for his birthday last month. The cobalt blue reminded her of his eyes, and when their gazes met, Faith's heart skipped a beat.

It was an involuntary reaction. And an unsettling one. If

she didn't know any better, Faith would've called it attraction. But that was impossible. She and Chase had been friends practically since birth. Romance had never been a part of their relationship, for good reason. They were too different.

An adrenaline junkie, Chase was fond of dirt bike racing and scary movies. He pushed boundaries and charmed naysayers with a flick of his dimple and an easygoing smile. Every single woman in the county was vying for his attention. He carried a bad boy edge tempered only by age and some hard-earned wisdom. The police officer's uniform didn't hurt either.

Faith was social and chatty with friends, but she was an introvert at heart. Reading was her main source of entertainment, and a quiet evening at home with a cup of tea and a good book was all she needed. She was serious, organized, and the ultimate rule-follower. Boring with a capital B in dating terms. Especially for someone like Chase.

No, they were excellent friends, but anything more...it was a recipe for disaster.

Faith tamped down the flutters in her stomach as Chase crossed the room toward her. She was just lonely. Christmastime made it worse, a reminder of all that she'd lost over the last several years. Her husband. Their potential family. She was absolutely not attracted to her best friend. The idea was simply preposterous.

Clinging to the thought, Faith turned her attention to the problem at hand. "Did you find anything new?"

"No. We've done a canvass of the woods but didn't recover any new evidence. There's no sign of the baby's mom or your attacker." Chase stopped in front of Faith, his gaze dropping to the infant in her arms. A smile curled at the corners of his mouth. "She's beautiful."

"She is." Faith touched the curve of the little girl's cheek. She had wide blue eyes that radiated with innocence. Hair, the color of hay, curled at the edges of her dainty ears and dusted across her forehead. Judging from her size and weight, she was about two months old. "I think her name is Anna."

Faith lifted the edge of the blanket wrapped around the baby so Chase could see the monogrammed letters etched on the fabric. "This looks handmade, but I don't recognize the needlework. I don't think it was bought from any of the stores in town, but it might be worth asking at the Sewing Circle."

The Sewing Circle was the only craft store for thirty miles. Betty, the owner, had been running the place since Faith was in diapers and knew every seamstress in the area. If anyone could recognize the stitching, it would be her.

Chase nodded. "Worth a shot. Is the sheriff in here?"

"He's talking to Holly in the living room."

As if the conversation had called them, the couple entered the kitchen. Sheriff Aiden James wore a serious expression that matched the broad stride of his steps and the crispness of his uniform. Beside him, Holly Miller looked delicate, although she was anything but. As a social worker, she fought day and night to help the citizens of Cutler. Aiden and Holly had met last Christmas, fell in love, and gotten married. They made a good couple, and Faith was blessed to consider them both friends.

Holly's blonde hair was pulled back into a low ponytail, and she offered Faith a gentle smile. She gestured toward the empty bottle on the kitchen table. "I see Anna didn't have any problems eating."

Faith patted the baby's back. "Not a bit. Poor thing was starving after being examined by the paramedics. I'm glad you brought basic supplies with you. Formula and diapers aren't things I normally have on hand."

"If only everything were so easy to fix..." Holly glanced at her husband and then focused back on Faith and Chase. "We have a problem. I've called all the foster families on my roster, but no one can take Anna."

Faith sank into a kitchen chair. She hugged the baby closer, relishing the sweet burden in her arms. "What will happen to her?"

"I was hoping you could take her for a few days."

Shock vibrated through Faith, followed by a sudden panic. She felt the blood drain from her face. Children were a soft spot for her, and she kept the walls around her heart intact at work because those kids had loving parents and wonderful homes. But Anna...already the baby was wriggling into Faith's heart and it'd only been a few hours. "Me?"

"That's a terrible idea," Chase snapped. His handsome face was twisted into a scowl. "We don't know how the baby ended up here or who attacked Faith. Leaving Anna in her care puts them both at risk."

"They may both be at risk no matter what we do." Aiden placed his hands on the duty belt at his hips. "The fact that none of the foster families can take Anna may be a blessing in disguise. This isn't a large county. If the man who attacked Faith was after the baby, it wouldn't be difficult for him to find Anna. He can simply ask around to find out who in town suddenly appeared at the grocery store with a new baby, looking for formula."

Faith's heart stuttered at the thought. "The foster family could be in danger, including any other children staying with them."

Aiden nodded. "Exactly. Keeping Anna with you means we can have police protection on you both, should it be necessary. It also buys us time to sort out what happened to her mom."

"Do you really think the attacker will come back?"

"Statically, it's unlikely. But the viciousness of the assault on you worries me." Aiden passed a glance toward his wife. "I've learned the hard way that desperation can push a criminal to the brink. I'd rather be overcautious than not."

Last Christmas, Holly had been attacked and nearly killed. The incident was a stark reminder that even in small towns, danger could lurk. Aiden's concern could be a byproduct of the experience, but he wasn't one to be overly dramatic. Faith's heart sank as the reality of the situation seeped into her. This morning's traumatic event had been enough for a lifetime. She didn't want to spend the next days or weeks fearful the attacker would come back.

As if reading the turn of her thoughts, Chase placed a reassuring hand on Faith's shoulder. "You won't be alone for a minute. I've already rescheduled my plans to attend the wedding this weekend. I'm sticking by your side until the attacker is caught."

"And we'll amp up patrols around this area of town," Aiden added. "We're also going to put every available resource possible into finding little Anna's mom. I'm hopeful we'll know more in a few days."

Relief softened the sharp edges of her fear. Faith focused on the baby in her arms and her chest squeezed tight. The sweet thing had fallen back to sleep. Long lashes rested on plump cheeks, and her rosebud mouth moved in a soft sucking motion, as if she was dreaming of her next bottle. "How long would Anna stay with me?"

The kitchen chair scraped against the tile floor as Holly joined Faith at the table. "Through the holidays. I know it's a lot to ask, Faith, but I don't have many other options. Legally, Anna's temporary placement has to be registered and approved as a foster parent, which you are."

Faith nodded, gently hugging the baby closer to her. "Mitch and I wanted to have a family. He'd been adopted and wanted to forward that blessing to other children. It was something we were both passionate about."

An unexpected wave of grief rolled over her. They'd had so many dreams, an entire lifetime of them. Sensing her sadness, Scamp trotted over from the window and rested his head on Faith's lap. She gently nudged him away from sniffing Anna's blanket and gave the old dog's ears a gentle rub. "After Mitch died, I asked to be removed from the list of potential foster care parents. I wasn't in the right headspace to do it alone."

"Understandably." Chase squeezed her shoulder, the touch familiar and comforting. Concern rode the hard line of his mouth. "You don't have to do this, Faith. None of us would blame you if you said no."

He doubted her strength. Faith didn't fault him for it. She'd been something of a wreck since her husband's death, operating on autopilot most of the time, and Chase knew her love of children ran bone-deep. It would hurt to let Anna go when the danger was over, but Faith couldn't send her away any more than she could cut off her own arm. It wasn't who she was.

"I want to help." She straightened her spine, resolve fueling her words. "Anna's staying with me."

FOUR

First Steps Daycare was nestled in the heart of town on Main Street. Originally a house, it'd been converted into a child's paradise. Beautiful murals in bold colors decorated every wall, soft rubber flooring provided padding for unfortunate falls, and a fenced backyard, complete with a sturdy wooden swing set, provided outdoor activity. Rooms were divided by age and an array of appropriate toys provided.

Chase rubbed his temples, a headache brewing behind his forehead. He'd spent the last five hours at the front desk, working alongside Faith and keeping an eye on both her and little Anna. "How on earth do you handle all the noise?"

The daycare was blessedly quiet now that the last child had left, but the sounds of laughter, playful screams, and more than a bit of crying had filled the space during business hours. The last employee had left fifteen minutes ago, but Faith hadn't stopped moving all day. She was currently filing papers, Anna strapped to her chest in a sling.

Faith made everything look effortless. No one would've guessed she'd been viciously attacked this morning or that she'd spent the entire afternoon running a hectic business while caring for a child that'd been dropped in her lap unexpectedly. She was amazing.

She cast Chase a glance out of the corner of her eye and a pretty smile curved the edges of her mouth. "You chase down criminals and dodge bullets, but can't handle a few crying kids? There's aspirin in the medicine cabinet, tough guy."

He scowled at her when she tossed him the keys. He found the right one for the medicine cabinet and fished out the painkillers. "Laugh all you want, but I'd rather take the graveyard shift on patrol than work here full-time. Crying, wailing, screaming...I've never seen so many tears in all my life."

Faith laughed. "Little ones are passionate." She shut the filing cabinet with a bump of her hip. "Okay, that was the last of it. We can get out of here, although I need to stop by the grocery store on my way home. The formula and diapers Holly brought over this morning won't be enough to get me through the weekend."

"No problem." Chase downed the medication.

He extended his hand, offering the keys back to Faith, and was surprised when she grasped his fingers after taking them. She lifted her gaze to meet his. "In case I forgot to tell you, thanks. I know you were looking forward to the wedding this weekend, and spending hours at the daycare, watching over me and Anna today wasn't much fun."

Warmth spread through Chase, fueled by the silkiness of her skin against his and the softness in her eyes. His heart skipped several beats, and it took him a minute to remember how to talk. "I was just grumbling about the noise. It wasn't horrible being here today."

Any time he could spend with Faith was fine with him. She was his favorite person to be around, but that dipped too close into dangerous territory. Chase flashed her a grin, hoping to mask the flare of attraction racing through him. "But if you're looking for a way to really thank me, think brownies. Chocolate ones with nuts and caramel."

She shook her head, hair fluttering around her shoulders, and laughed. Faith unwrapped Anna from the sling and carefully placed her in a car seat Holly had loaned them. "Get out of here, Chase. I'm not baking anything."

"Come on." He grabbed the playpen and sack of toys by the door. The items belonged to the daycare, but Faith was borrowing them for the weekend. "I'll make you a deal. I'll grill steaks for dinner tonight, and you bake brownies tomorrow."

"Now you're talking. That's a deal."

Chase placed a hand on Faith's arm, preventing her from opening the front door. He peered into the street. Most of the shops were still open, residents bustling from one place to another. Twinkling Christmas lights flashed in the store windows. Chase's truck was sitting in front of the daycare. Nothing appeared out of the ordinary.

Faith stiffened underneath his palm. "What is it?"

"Just being cautious." Chase offered her a reassuring smile before opening the front door. So far, the day had been uneventful, but he'd done periodic patrols of the immediate area around the daycare. Each time, Chase had wrestled with the sensation of being watched.

Even now, as he hustled Faith and Anna to the car, the back of his neck prickled. Imagination or instincts, Chase couldn't be sure. The attack from this morning bothered him far more than he let on. A thorough search of the surrounding land around Faith's property hadn't yielded any new evidence. There was no sign of Anna's mother, and they were no closer to identifying her. Chase couldn't shake the feeling that something terrible had happened to the woman.

He breathed a sigh of relief once everyone was nestled inside the vehicle. The grocery store was ten minutes away, on the other side of town. Faith pointed out various Christmas decorations along the way. Chase enjoyed listening to her chatter on, the lilt of her voice soothing his headache into submission.

"Have you finished your Christmas shopping?" Faith asked.

"Yep. I bought my mom's present yesterday. I took your suggestion and got that purple sweater you found online." Chase arched his brows. "You know, I'm pretty sure she figured out a long time ago that you're the one actually selecting the presents I buy. I should just put your name on the card."

"Don't you dare. Besides, it's reciprocal. I never would've found the right drill for my dad without your help."

"Did you tell your parents about this morning?"

She sighed. "Yes. They're worried, but I explained that you'll be watching out for me and that made them feel better. They're having a great time on the church trip. I hated to spoil it, but I was worried your mom would say something, and figured the news was better coming from me."

"You're right. Oh, by the way, my mom is working, but she'd love to stop by and have breakfast with us tomorrow morning. Do you mind?"

Chase's mom was a nurse and worked at the local emergency clinic. Like Faith, he'd hesitated to tell his mom about the attack this morning, since Maggie McKenzie was a natural worrier, but keeping the assault quiet was impossible. In Cutler, news traveled faster than birds could fly. At least if his mom heard the news from Chase, he could provide the facts and temper her concerns.

"Of course your mom can come for breakfast. I would love that." Faith rubbed her hands together with excitement. "I'll make pancakes. Those are her favorite."

Despite teasing about the brownies earlier, Faith loved to cook for other people. She had a way of making everyone feel at home around her. Knowing his mom was coming over, she would probably make more than pancakes. It would be a breakfast buffet by the time Faith was done.

Anna sent up whimpers of protest as Chase pulled into the grocery store parking lot. He glanced at the little one tucked in her car seat behind the passenger seat. "Is she okay?"

Faith hopped out of the truck and unstrapped the baby. She winced. "Blowout."

Chase gasped as she lifted Anna. Goop covered the baby's clothes, extending from the middle of her back all the way down her legs. "How can so much stuff come out of someone so little?"

"Grab the diaper bag. We're going to have to do damage control inside."

He did as she requested, snagging the carrier as well since it was also soiled. Faith hurried across the parking lot several strides ahead of him. She spoke in a soothing voice to the baby, the sound carrying on the wind although the actual words were indistinct. Anna fussed, legs wriggling, as she protested her dirty diaper. Chase caught up to them as they entered the grocery store.

It smelled of floor cleaner and freshly baked cookies inside. Beeps from the registers mingled with the soft voices of customers and the squeaks of shopping cart wheels. The restrooms were tucked next to a small pharmacy. Faith paused outside the door. "I'll get Anna cleaned up first and then we can deal with the car seat."

"Sounds like a plan." Chase hooked the diaper bag over her shoulder. Anna blew a raspberry as they disappeared into the restroom and he couldn't help but laugh. Even covered in such a mess, she was adorable. It tugged on his heartstrings unexpectedly.

He'd never considered marriage or a family seriously. At least…not until recently. It was sitting in the church, watching Faith swear to honor and cherish another man that'd forced Chase to face a reality he'd been running from for a long time.

He loved Faith. He'd loved her beyond what he thought was possible.

Chase spent the next two years dating, hoping his feelings for Faith were simply a misdirected desire to settle down with his own life partner. But no one he ever went out with interested him. No one could because none of those women were Faith.

And now...now she was a widow, but her heart still belonged to Mitch.

He leaned against the wall beside the bathroom door, keeping watch on the customers moving throughout the store. The evening rush had begun. Every passing minute brought more people in, and the lines at the register grew longer. It made Chase uncomfortable. Keeping Anna and Faith safe was harder in a crowd.

He glanced at his watch. They'd been in the bathroom for over ten minutes. Chase knocked on the door before pushing it open slightly. "Faith, everything okay?"

Silence. His heart skipped a beat as he raised his voice. "Faith, I'm coming in."

He shoved open the door. The diaper-changing station was lowered, Anna's soiled clothes resting in a pile nearby. Water ran from a faucet into the sink, as if someone had been interrupted while washing their hands, and the only stall was empty. Anna's diaper bag was a bright blot of color against the silver paper towel dispenser. Horror ripped through Chase.

The bathroom was empty. Faith and the baby were gone.

FIVE

The barrel of the gun jabbed into Faith's kidney, sending pain shooting along her back. Faith ignored it. She clutched Anna close to her chest, her gaze scanning the empty alley behind the grocery store, desperate for someone to come out and notice them being dragged away by the man in the ski mask. But there was no one. Evening had given way to night, and although the grocery store parking lot was busy, darkness shrouded them.

Faith berated herself for letting down her guard. She'd been consumed with cleaning up the baby and hadn't noticed the attacker coming in through another door in the rear of the bathroom—the same one he'd used to drag her out of the grocery store. Her muffled cries had gone unnoticed—thanks to the tape covering her mouth—and she couldn't fight off the attacker, not with Anna in her arms.

She dragged her feet, attempting to slow their progression to the other side of the alley where a silver truck waited. Her kidnapper jabbed his gun into her kidney again, hard enough to leave a large bruise. His grip on her arm felt like a vise.

"Move it," he growled.

His voice was harsh and barely discernible over the roar of Faith's own heartbeat. The truck loomed large. Everything was happening too quickly. She had to figure out a way to delay, to give Chase time to realize she was missing. Anna stirred against her chest. Who knew what their kidnapper would do to the sweet baby? Faith had to protect her at all costs.

There was only one option she could think of. Prayers in her heart, Faith melted to the cold ground, catching the attacker off guard. He nearly tripped over Faith. His iron grasp on her bicep loosened. She scrambled to back away from him while keeping Anna safe, but her movements were ungainly.

The attacker's arm rose and then came down quickly. Pain exploded through Faith's skull as the butt of the gun collided with her head. She toppled onto her back. By the grace of God, she managed to keep her arms around Anna, preventing the child from tumbling to the hard ground. Stars danced across Faith's vision. She felt, rather than saw, the attacker grab her arm again.

In the distance, a door slammed against something. A shout emanated from the other side of the alley. Chase!

"Police!" His voice was authoritative. "Freeze!"

The attacker dropped Faith's arm, and for a blessed moment, she thought it was over. Then his rough hands wrapped around little Anna. He tried to pull the baby away.

Faith yelled, her shout muffled by the tape around her

mouth. Blood from the injury to her scalp ran down her forehead into her eyes. She clung to Anna, blindly kicking out, attempting to do everything possible to stop him. The infant's screams tore at her heart. She feared the tug-of-war was hurting her, but letting the kidnapper escape with Anna wasn't an option. Not while Faith had breath still left in her body.

Footsteps pounded down the alley. The kidnapper glanced over his shoulder and then released Anna. He took off. Seconds later, the truck's engine turned over and he peeled out of the alley.

Faith collapsed against the asphalt, sobs rising in her chest as she hugged Anna close. She couldn't breathe. She ripped the tape from her mouth. Tears streamed down her face as she ran her hands over the baby, checking her for obvious injuries. There were none.

Chase crouched next to them. His gun was in one hand and his gaze swept over her and the baby. "You're hurt. How bad?"

She couldn't answer his question, emotions overwhelming her. Chase tucked his gun back into its holster and tore off his jacket and then his shirt. He wore an undershirt beneath. It molded to the hard planes of his chest.

"You're bleeding." His tone was angry, but as Chase pressed the fabric to her hairline, his touch was tender. Faith was tempted to sink into his embrace, but she pushed off his concern for her welfare. Anna was more important. The baby's cries had quieted to a whimper, but that didn't matter. She could be seriously injured from the attack.

Faith struggled to her feet. "He tried to kidnap Anna.

We need to get her to the hospital and make sure she's okay."

Half an hour later, she hovered over the exam table at the emergency clinic as Dr. Robert Whitcomb examined the baby. Anna wore nothing but a diaper. Faint redness marred her soft skin, the marks in the shape of large fingers. The sight of them churned Faith's stomach. On the other side of the room, Chase stood sentry. His expression was hard, but worry lurked in the depths of his eyes.

Robert gently palpated Anna's tummy. Mid-thirties and handsome, he'd moved to town last year after losing his wife to cancer. Faith didn't know him well, but his son attended her daycare. Robert was an attentive father, and so far, seemed to carry that same trait to his work. He checked Anna's reflexes and did a few more things Faith couldn't name. She chewed on a fingernail as he shined a light into the baby's eyes.

Chase pushed off the wall and came to Faith's side. He tugged her hand down from her mouth and interlaced their fingers. She leaned into his touch, letting her head rest against the chiseled line of his shoulder. He was her rock.

"Well, everything looks fine." Robert clicked off the tiny flashlight. "I don't see any cause for concern. These marks on her tummy may deepen into bruises, so be careful when handling her since they may be sore to the touch, but otherwise Anna is perfectly healthy."

Faith's breath caught. "Are you sure? I was holding on to her so tightly—" Tears burned behind her eyelids as the memory of the attack washed over her. It'd been an impossible situation. Let Anna go and risk the kidnapper escaping with her, or fight to hold on and potentially injure her.

"I'm positive." Robert lifted Anna off the exam table. "Babies are surprisingly resilient."

Relief washed over Faith, the emotion so heady her knees weakened. "Thank you, God."

"Amen." Chase eased her onto the examination table. "Now it's your turn to be looked at. That head wound might need stitches." He turned toward Robert. "Dr. Whitcomb, you can give Anna to me."

The other man didn't move. Faith glanced at him. There was a strange look on Robert's face as he gazed down at the child in his arms. It sent a chill of apprehension through her veins. She reached for Anna.

Her movements seemed to jostle Robert back into the present, because the look melted away and a smile replaced it. "Sorry, I got lost there for a minute, remembering when my son was this little. It goes by so fast."

Faith blinked. What on earth... The knock to her head must've scrambled her brain more than she'd thought. Robert didn't have anything to do with the attacks on her. Her imagination was running away with itself, a side effect of having her life threatened twice within twenty-four hours.

A cell phone beeped. Robert shook his head. "That's mine. Please excuse me for a moment. I'll be right back."

He handed Chase the baby and then left the room. The door swung shut behind him. Faith took a deep breath—her first since the attack—and her shoulders dropped. Anna looked so small next to Chase's broad shoulders. She still wasn't wearing any clothes, and Faith handed him a blanket. "Here, she'll get cold. Do you want me to wrap her?"

"I've got it." He laid her down on the table next to Faith

and quickly swaddled the baby. Chase winked. "All those years of babysitting alongside you when we were teenagers paid off in the end."

She chuckled. "I knew you'd thank me one day."

The smile melted from her face as she studied him. Chase's hands were huge against Anna's tiny form, but his movements were gentle and caring. He'd never gotten close to marriage or kids, but Faith had sensed a subtle shift in him lately. A desire to settle down, maybe?

"You'll make an amazing dad, Chase."

Surprise sent his eyebrows winging upward. "You think so?"

Faith's heart tumbled in her chest. She hadn't realized he had doubts about himself in those areas. Chase always seemed...well, so confident and self-assured. Then again, his father had abandoned the family when Chase was eight. That had to have left a mark.

She placed a hand on his arm. "I know so."

Before she could say any more, the door to the exam room opened and Maggie bustled in. Chase's mom wore blue scrubs and her dark hair was pulled into a high ponytail. She carried an ice pack in one hand. Worry etched lines in her forehead, but she plastered on a smile. "How are we doing in here?"

Chase tucked Anna into the crook of his arm. "We're waiting on Dr. Whitcomb to examine Faith, but he gave Anna a clean bill of health."

"Well, thank goodness for that." Maggie yanked several paper towels from the wall dispenser and wrapped them around the ice pack before handing it to Faith. "Put that on your head, hon. It'll help with the swelling. Any dizziness? Nausea?"

"No, I'm just exhausted. It's been a long day." Now that she knew for sure Anna was okay, the adrenaline was seeping out of her system. Every muscle in her body ached, and her head was pounding.

Maggie nodded, her expression sympathetic. "I'll do my best to hurry Dr. Whitcomb along so you guys can get home. Don't worry about breakfast tomorrow morning. I'll pick up something for all of us on my way over." She wrapped her arms around Faith in a motherly embrace. "I'm so glad you're okay, hon." Maggie backed off, reaching for her son. "All of you."

The move caused a fresh wave of emotion to swell inside Faith. She didn't want to think about what could've happened. The danger hadn't been restricted to herself and Anna. The kidnapper had a gun. He could've shot Chase when he arrived to rescue them. It was a terrifying realization and one that cut too closely to a familiar scar on her heart. Faith had already lost her husband. She couldn't imagine losing her best friend too.

God, please watch over all of us. Especially Chase and Anna.

Things weren't over. Faith knew that without a doubt. Any man desperate enough to attempt kidnapping her from a public place wasn't going to slink back into the shadows. It wasn't a matter of if he would try again...

It was a matter of when.

SIX

Chase hauled hay into the horse stall and scattered it on the ground. Sweat beaded on his brow as his muscles worked, but the exercise didn't erase the rough edges of his anger. Faith's head wound had required ten stitches. She and Anna had nearly been kidnapped.

And all of it had happened on his watch.

Experience and maturity had changed him from the reckless teenage boy he'd once been. Chase took his job as a police officer seriously, and while he'd vowed to protect everyone in town, that Faith was the one in danger only added an extra layer to the case. He'd screwed up today. He wouldn't let it happen again.

Chase brought Poppy in from the pasture and then filled her food and water buckets before heading out into the frigid night air. The chickens were hunkered down in their coop. Scamper loped next to him as they crossed the yard to the house. The lights in the kitchen were glowing. Through the bay window, Faith was visible. She was feeding Anna a bottle.

Chase's steps faltered. His heart clenched tightly in his chest. Man, she was beautiful. Faith's gorgeous hair flowed over her shoulders in a waterfall, and the look on her face as she gazed down at the baby in her arms...it was pure joy. For half a moment, Chase allowed himself to imagine that was their child she was holding. Her comment at the hospital rolled through his mind.

You'll make an amazing dad.

It'd surprised him to learn Faith thought so. Despite their close bond, his dating life wasn't something they'd ever discussed. Maybe because he'd always been so clear that marriage and a family weren't what he wanted. His own father hadn't bothered to stick around, and that fact had left a sour taste in Chase's mouth when it came to commitment. Why bother when it wasn't real anyway? Deep down, he didn't expect anyone to stick it out. The idea was so ingrained, he'd purposefully avoided getting serious with any of his girlfriends. A decision he'd been absolutely convinced was the right one...until Faith was standing at the altar marrying Mitch.

A twig snapped, drawing Chase out of his thoughts. He spun. His hand flew to his weapon and Scamper growled in warning.

Aiden stepped out of the shadows, the police badge pinned to his uniform glimmering in the porch light. "It's only me. Sorry if I startled you."

Chase relaxed. Aiden and Holly had arrived half an hour ago, loaded down with enough groceries to last a month. The men had left Holly and Faith locked inside the house. While Chase was tending the animals, Aiden patrolled the property.

"Everything okay?" Chase asked, lowering his hand to scratch Scamper behind the ears. The old dog leaned into his touch.

"All clear. But I received a phone call from David."

David Carpenter was another officer in the police department. Smart and capable, he'd been aiding Aiden with the investigation, and Chase trusted David implicitly. They'd grown up together.

Chase's hand stilled against Scamper's soft fur. "And?"

Aiden's expression was haunted. "The tip Faith gave us about the stitching on Anna's blanket paid off. We've identified Anna's mother. Her name is Hillary Evans. She's missing and has been since the night before Faith found Anna in her barn."

Chase's heart sank to his feet. That didn't bode well for Hillary. He took a deep breath and let it out slowly. "The name sounds familiar to me. Is she a resident of Cutler?"

"She used to be." Aiden hunched inside his jacket. "Let's go in and discuss things. I think it'll be good to involve Faith and Holly in the conversation."

The men went inside. The warmth of the kitchen was inviting, but the smile Faith shot Chase was more so. He quickly washed his hands. The scent of steaks grilling on the stove made his stomach growl. Holly and Aiden kissed before sharing teasing remarks about Holly's cooking.

As if his feet had a mind of their own, Chase crossed the room to Faith. Her complexion was pale and there was a faint scratch on her cheek. Evidence of the attack from this evening. He lightly touched her back, giving in to his need for physical contact with Faith, before dragging his gaze from her beautiful face to the baby in her arms. "How's Anna?"

"She's a champion eater." Faith removed the empty bottle from between Anna's lips. The little girl had drifted to sleep. "I hate to move her, but if she doesn't burp, we'll pay the price later."

"I'll do it."

Faith needed a break. She'd been through a lot in the last twenty-four hours. Chase took the burp cloth from the table and tossed it over his shoulder. He gently lifted Anna and placed her against his chest before lightly patting her back. It felt surprisingly normal and natural to hold the baby. Her weight was slight, no more than a sack of flour, and when she snuggled against him with a sigh, affection spread through his chest.

Chase fought against the temptation to daydream. Anna didn't belong to him. Or Faith. The baby was only in their lives temporarily, and then things would go back to the way they used to be.

After Anna had burped, he forced himself to place her in the portable crib next to the dining table. Faith covered her with a blanket. The next few minutes were spent organizing dinner. Holly and Faith had put together a great meal. Along with the steaks, there was a salad, rolls, and twice-baked potatoes. Once grace was said and everyone had begun eating, Aiden shared what he'd learned about Anna's mother.

Faith gasped, her hand flying to her mouth. "Hillary? She worked for me but quit in February. She took a job in Austin and moved away."

Chase's hand tightened on his fork. He knew the name

was familiar for a reason. Faith's comment jogged his memory. Hillary was a petite brunette with a sunny disposition. He'd only met her once or twice when dropping off or picking up something from the daycare for Faith. "Have you had any contact with her recently?"

"None. She didn't work for me for very long. Only about six months." Faith's attention shot to the baby sleeping in the crib and her brow creased. "Dr. Whitcomb believes Anna is about eight weeks old. If that's correct, then Hillary would've been pregnant when she left town."

"Maybe that's the reason she moved." Chase met Aiden's gaze across the table. He could see his own suspicions reflected in his boss's expression. Could Anna's father be the person behind these attacks? It was a likely scenario. "Do you know if Hillary was dating anyone in the months or weeks before she moved?"

Faith shook her head. "We didn't discuss her personal life much. Why? What are you thinking?"

"It's possible Hillary moved away to hide her pregnancy. She came back to speak to the father and ended up in some kind of altercation." Chase turned over the possibilities in his mind. "Unfortunately, there's a lot we don't know. Like where she is now. And how she and Anna ended up on your property."

Aiden frowned. "The road running alongside Faith's property is a shortcut across town. If we assume Hillary and Anna were in a car, it's possible the attacker was driving. We found tire tracks embedded in the dirt. Someone took that route after the rainstorm."

Chase nodded, catching up to Aiden's train of thought. "Let's assume Hillary, Anna, and the perpetrator were in a car together. There's a fight or an altercation. Hillary hops out of the vehicle with Anna and starts running. She's lost and desperate."

"Why not just run up to the house?" Holly asked. "The porch lights are bright enough to be seen."

Chase considered the question. The image of the footprints in Faith's yard flashed in his mind. "She headed that way, but her attacker was too close. She diverted to the barn. Maybe to hide. She might've been hoping he would assume she went to the house."

"Except he wasn't fooled." Faith's voice was hollow. "He followed Hillary into the barn and attacked her. Then he carried her back to his car before returning to the barn for Anna."

Chase placed a hand over Faith's. He didn't like to think about how close she'd come to losing her life. There was no doubt in his mind that the attacker would've killed her, as he'd likely done with Hillary. "We should put out a BOLO for Hillary's car and list her as critically missing."

BOLO was short for be-on-the-lookout. Every officer in the state would be searching for Hillary's car. And for her.

Aiden nodded. "It's already done. I—"

Holly screamed. She jumped from her chair and pointed to the yard. Her whole body was shaking. "Someone's out there. I saw a face in the window."

Chase leapt to his feet. "Aiden, stay with them and call for backup."

He palmed his weapon and went out the back door. His boots thumped against the wood porch. The cold air cut through his thin T-shirt, but there wasn't time to grab a jacket. Every second counted. His gaze scanned the yard. A figure, barely discernible beyond the porch light, was streaking across the grass. Male. Dark clothes. He was headed for the tree line.

Oh no, you don't.

Chase bolted after him.

SEVEN

The intruder got away.

Faith rocked Anna gently back to sleep after her midmorning bottle. Silence settled around them, a welcoming change from the hectic beginning to the day. Aiden and Holly had stayed in the guest bedroom, helping to keep watch over Faith and the baby. Then Maggie, Chase's mom, had come by for breakfast.

All the guests had left fifteen minutes ago, and while Faith loved having people around, it could be overwhelming if she never got a break. The restless night of sleep she'd had didn't help. Every time she closed her eyes, she imagined Hillary running away from a faceless masked man. It was terrifying.

"Oh, Anna." The little one had drifted off to sleep, long lashes casting shadows on her cheeks. Faith gently set her in the playpen next to the couch—she kept Anna close to her at all times—and then gently ran a hand across the baby's hair. The strands were downy and soft. Like silk. "I know you must miss your mom. And wherever she is, I'm sure she's missing you too."

Faith didn't want to believe Hillary was dead. Not yet. Not without proof.

Chase appeared in the doorway. His hair was damp from a shower and his jaw was clean-shaven. The scent of his cologne wafted in Faith's direction. She breathed it in, letting the leathery scent soothe the rough edges of her nerves. It drifted through her mind that she didn't consider Chase to be an intrusion on her quiet. He was...well, he was Chase.

He smiled, the dimple in his left cheek winking. "You got her to sleep. I think you have the magic touch. She absolutely refused to go down after her bottle at 4 a.m. I spent two hours walking around the living room, talking to her."

"You should have woken me."

He shrugged. "You need rest. How's your head?"

"Fine." She absently touched the stitches buried in her hair. "A little achy, but nothing unmanageable."

Her heart did a pitter-patter when he joined her on the couch. Faith scooted closer, and Chase automatically wrapped his arm around her shoulders. She rested her head against his chest. The position was familiar, one they'd done hundreds of times over the years, but this time...this time, it was different.

Maybe because Faith was different.

She'd loved Mitch with all her heart. Marrying him had been the right thing to do, and losing him had cut her deeply. But these recent threats, Chase's protection, and taking care of Anna had opened her eyes to the truth. Faith wasn't living. Not really. She was standing still, watching life go by, and ignoring the blessings around her.

It had to stop. Yes, she'd lost her husband, and that was a tragedy. But Faith was still alive, and she needed to embrace that gift. It was time to decide what she wanted for herself, and that started with acknowledging this humming attraction for Chase. When it began, she couldn't say, but somewhere over the last two years, she'd developed feelings beyond friendship. Even now, every inch of her was acutely aware of Chase. The solid beat of his heart, the warmth of his hand, the strength of his muscles.

But did he feel the same way? Would saying something ruin their relationship? Did they even want the same things? Chase had been adamant about not wanting marriage and a family. There was no indication he'd changed his mind about that.

Maybe these pulls toward Chase were just a way of feeling something romantic for someone who would never reciprocate. A way to play it safe. Risking their friendship over an ill-advised romance was a terrible idea. Faith needed to tread lightly.

Anna whimpered in her sleep, and Faith gently rubbed her back. Tenderness swept over her. "When Mitch first brought up the idea of adoption, I'm ashamed to admit I was hesitant. I wasn't sure I'd be able to love someone else's baby with my whole heart. But I was wrong. Anna isn't even mine, but I would do anything to protect her. I could see myself easily falling in love with her."

It took superhuman effort not to. The situation was precarious, and it was too difficult to think beyond today.

Chase tilted his head. "It's hard to imagine you ever

having any misgivings about your capacity to love a child. It's obvious to everyone else that you're a natural caregiver, Faith."

"We all have our doubts." She pegged him with a look. "For the record, in case you needed to hear it, you deserve all the happiness in the world. I meant what I said yesterday in the hospital. You'd make a great dad. Husband, too, if you decide that's what you want."

An unexpected spark of jealousy flared at the thought of Chase marrying someone else. The intensity of it caught Faith off guard. A warning sign that her feelings might go deeper than even she wanted to admit.

Their eyes locked, and for a heart-stopping moment, Faith thought he'd been able to read the thoughts running through her mind. It pinned her in place. Her heart thundered in her chest, and she suddenly felt woozy.

Then his gaze slid away and Chase cleared his throat. "Thank you for saying so." His mouth quirked. "But please don't mention that to my mom. She'll have every single woman in the county chasing after me."

Faith rolled her eyes, letting out the breath she was holding. "I'm pretty sure they already are. Which you love. You've dated half the town." She arched her brow. "I'm surprised none of them have dragged you to the altar yet."

His grin faded as he met her gaze once more. "Maybe I'm just waiting for the right one."

She froze. There was something in his expression... Faith's pulse kicked up a notch as heat crept into her cheeks. No, it had to be a figment of her imagination. Chase couldn't possibly be interested in her. This absurd attraction humming through her was messing with her head.

Faith forced a bright smile. "Don't wait too long." She lightly punched his shoulder. "Your looks will fade eventually."

He brought a hand to his chest in mock pain. "Ouch. Way to burn a guy's ego."

They both laughed. The tension, real or imagined, eased from the room. Faith's shoulders dropped, and she smothered a yawn. "Anna has the right idea. I might take a nap—"

A knock at the front door cut her off. Scamper barked from his bed in the corner of the room. Chase immediately rose from the couch. "Are you expecting someone?"

"No, but I doubt cold-blooded killers knock on the door."

He waved off her comment, heading for the front door on long strides. His hand went to his weapon at his hip as he peeked out the dining room window. He frowned. "It's your neighbors. What are their names again?"

"Marsha and Tom Bradley. They own that car dealership off the freeway." Faith hurried across the room and was at Chase's side when he opened the door. She offered her neighbors a friendly smile. "Hi, guys."

Mid-thirties, Marsha was slender with naturally curly hair. Her husband, Tom, was over six-one and burly. A thick beard covered the bottom-half of his face. A brand-new SUV sparkled in the sunshine. The Bradleys always had the newest vehicles. Faith didn't know them well, but Tom's older kids—teenagers from his first marriage—tended her yard last summer to earn extra money for a school trip.

"I'm sorry to bother you, Faith." Marsha shoved her hands into the pockets of her peacoat. "But we heard a rumor in town that you'd found a baby in your barn and that the child might belong to Hillary Evans." Her gaze drifted to Chase. "If that's true, we may have some information about the case."

Faith wasn't surprised that the rumor mill was in full swing, but she was shocked to learn the Bradleys might have information about Hillary's disappearance. She gestured them inside. "Please, come out of the cold. Have a seat."

Marsha and Tom settled on the coach. Faith went through the motions of offering them something to eat or drink, but they both refused. Marsha zeroed in on Anna right away, cooing over the sleeping baby. Tom ignored her.

"I didn't know y'all were friendly with Hillary." Faith let Chase sit in the recliner and then she perched on the arm. "How did you know her?"

"She babysat for us three days a week and sometimes on the weekends." Marsha opened her coat and shrugged it off. "Our youngest, Jennie, is only four. We needed someone to watch her during the hours I was at the car dealership. Hillary came highly recommended. I was sad when she turned in her notice. Jennie adored her."

"Were you aware that Hillary was pregnant when she quit?" Chase asked.

"I was." Marsha sighed. "Hillary was excited to be a mom, but she refused to say who the dad was. I thought that was strange, especially since I'd seen her and Dr. Whitcomb having dinner together a few months before."

Faith stiffened. "Dr. Whitcomb? Hillary and Robert were dating?"

The memory of the way Robert looked at Anna in the

hospital flashed in Faith's mind. She'd dismissed it as nothing, but maybe she shouldn't have.

Tom straightened, laying a hand on his wife's arm. "Hold on. We need to be clear here, because I'm not comfortable accusing a man of something. Marsha isn't sure Dr. Whitcomb is the baby's father. Hillary never told us they were dating or involved."

Chase leaned forward. "Sir, this is an active investigation with a missing woman. Any information you have is helpful. No one is seeking to falsely accuse anyone. We simply want to locate Hillary and make sure she's okay."

Marsha blew out a breath. "Tell them, Tom. Tell them what you saw."

He scraped a hand over his beard. "A few days after my wife saw Dr. Whitcomb and Hillary together, I also spotted them. It was in a restaurant in the next town. I was there for a business meeting with a client who leases a lot of vehicles from us." Tom hesitated. "They were arguing in the parking lot. It got heated; so much so, I thought I was going to have to intervene. But then Hillary got into her car and drove away. Dr. Whitcomb left too. Neither of them saw me or knew I was there."

"Do you know what they were arguing about?" Chase asked.

"No. I was inside the restaurant and couldn't hear them."

Faith chewed on the inside of her cheek. "When you say it got heated, what does that mean?"

Tom swallowed hard. It was clear he was extremely uncomfortable sharing the information, which Faith could understand, but now was not the time to worry about gossip.

She clutched her hands together. "Please, Tom. This man has attacked me twice and attempted to kidnap Anna. Whoever he is, we need to find him before he can strike again."

Tom blew out a breath. "It looked like Dr. Whitcomb was going to hit her. He grabbed Hillary's arm, which is when I got up from my table and started to go outside. But by the time I got there, Hillary was already inside her car."

"Did you ever ask her about it?"

He met her gaze, and the look in his eyes was haunted. "No, but I should have. It was a mistake not to. And now I'll have to live with that decision for the rest of my life."

EIGHT

The Cutler Police Department was tucked between the courthouse and a coffee shop in the center of town. On the other side of the block, the main square bustled with activity. The Christmas Fair kicked off tonight. It was an annual event complete with carols, a tree-lighting ceremony, and fun games for the children. Booths were being set up for vendors and a stage was half-assembled for the choir.

Chase kept his senses alert as he escorted Faith and Anna across the street toward the police department entrance. Overprotective, perhaps, but the man who'd attacked them at the grocery store had done so in broad daylight. He wouldn't underestimate the criminal again.

Faith cast a wistful glance at the main square while pushing Anna in the stroller. "I wish we could attend the festivities tonight. The Christmas Fair is always so much fun."

"I'm sorry to miss it, too, but it's not safe. The crowds will make it impossible to keep you and Anna protected."

"No, you're right. I shouldn't complain. The main

priority is keeping Anna safe." Faith smiled down at the baby. "Isn't she the most precious thing you've ever seen?"

She was. Inside the stroller, Anna waved her tiny hands, blue eyes wide as she studied the black-and-white mobile hanging above her. She wore an oversized bow that made her look like a present. Even given the serious circumstances, the sight of Anna brought a smile to Chase's face. She was such a good baby. Happy and easygoing...that is, unless she was hungry. Then watch out. She had a healthy set of lungs on her.

They'd spent the last few days holed up in Faith's house while Aiden worked hard on the investigation. If you'd asked Chase before the experience, hunkering down with a baby would've been last on his list for welcomed experiences. But the reality was better than he could've ever imagined. And there was no doubt in his mind, Faith was the reason. Being with her, taking care of Anna together, had been like falling into a life he hadn't known existed, but somehow came naturally.

His heart was in dangerous territory. Every second with Faith only made his feelings for her stronger. He was teetering on the edge of a very painful heartbreak when this case was over. Chase knew it. But he was also powerless to stop it.

Which is why his stomach hadn't stopped churning since receiving Aiden's phone call this morning. His boss had some developments in the case and wanted to speak with them. Chase desperately wanted Faith and Anna out of danger, but he wasn't looking forward to losing the closeness they'd developed.

Chase held the door to the police department open for

Faith. The scent of her perfume teased his senses as she passed by. Her hair flowed loose around her shoulders like a silky curtain, and the cold winter air had put color in her cheeks. He wrestled with the urge to place a hand on the small of her back as they signed in and headed for Aiden's office.

The police station had a main area with cubicles for the officers. Twinkling lights flashed from every available surface. Garland was strung from the ceiling, marching across the wide room over the officer's desks. A tree, its branches burdened with ornaments and tinsel, glittered in the corner. Chase stopped midstep, his mouth dropping open. "Wow, that's a lot of Christmas decor."

Holly hurried across the room toward them. She was dressed in a Santa sweater, complete with flying reindeer. "I know, I know. I went overboard with the Christmas decorations. I can't help myself."

"They're beautiful." Faith smiled, her eyes bright with happiness. "You've inspired me to put up my tree. I'm sorry to say I've been neglectful in that area."

Chase's brows arched slightly, surprise rippling through him. Faith always decorated the outside of her house, but never pulled the tree down from the attic. He offered last year, but she refused, and he hadn't pushed. Her lack of Christmas cheer was connected to Mitch's death. Was it possible she was ready to move on?

Cool it, McKenzie. Decorating a Christmas tree was a far cry from dating. Over the last few days, there had been moments...subtle looks or slight touches that made Chase wonder if his feelings for Faith ran both ways. But he wouldn't allow himself to even hope. Especially not now.

Faith's life was being threatened. The last thing she needed was for Chase to complicate their relationship.

Holly tucked her hair behind her ears and bent over the stroller. "Anna, you look so pretty. I just love that bow you're wearing." She straightened, and the joy in her expression melted. "Aiden's waiting for you both in his office. Why don't you leave Anna here with me? I'll babysit while y'all talk."

The news couldn't be good. Faith must've come to the same conclusion because some of the color drained from her cheeks. She reached for Chase's hand, and he interlocked their fingers. Together, they went into Aiden's office and settled into the visitor's chairs.

Chase's muscles tightened at the look on his boss's face, and dread sat like a rock in the pit of his stomach. "You've found Hillary."

Aiden nodded. "Hikers located a body in Grayson Park yesterday afternoon. I received confirmation from the coroner this morning. It's Hillary. According to the autopsy, she was strangled. The estimated time of death coincides with the morning Anna was found in the barn."

Faith closed her eyes. "I was praying things would turn out differently."

Chase squeezed her hand. "We all were." He turned toward his boss. "Have you interviewed Dr. Whitcomb about his relationship with Hillary?"

"Yes." Aiden had dark circles under his eyes, a testament to how hard he was working on this case. "He claims they dated briefly but broke up months ago. His explanation coordinates with the times that Tom and Marsha Bradley spotted them out."

"That doesn't mean he isn't Anna's father."

"No, but I checked with the hospital. Dr. Whitcomb clocked in at six o'clock on Friday night, so he couldn't have attacked Faith and Anna in the grocery store parking lot. It doesn't rule him out completely—he could've hired someone—but I'm inclined to believe he's not involved."

Chase didn't know whether to be relieved or disappointed by the turn of events. "So that puts us back to square one?"

"Not exactly." Aiden clicked on a tablet and tapped the screen before turning it toward Chase and Faith. "Have either of you ever seen this man before?"

Chase leaned over to study the image. It was a mug shot. The guy stared into the camera with a cold expression. His wheat-colored hair was sticking up in all directions and there were smudges of dirt on his cheek. A nasty cut, fresh but not bleeding, rode the line of his brow. A memory niggled the back of Chase's mind.

Faith shook her head. "I haven't seen him before." She glanced at Chase. "You?"

He frowned. "He may have been walking on the sidewalk near the daycare Friday afternoon. There was a guy with a dark hat and blue jeans, but he was far away..." Chase closed his eyes, trying to envision the man in his mind, but the picture was unclear. He shook his head. "Sorry, Aiden. There were a lot of people out doing Christmas shopping. I can't swear it was him."

"Who is he?" Faith asked.

"Silas Evans, Hillary's brother." Aiden leaned back in his chair. "He's bad news. Silas has been arrested a few times for assault, domestic violence, and driving while under the influence. He lives in Austin and, according to the daycare Hillary was working for at the time she died, is her closest living relative. Their parents are deceased."

Chase turned over the new information. "Does he have a motive to want his sister dead?"

"Unfortunately, yes. Hillary inherited a substantial sum of money from her grandmother last year shortly before she moved to Austin. Silas didn't receive a penny. According to Hillary's friends, her brother was angry about it. Neighbors in her apartment complex witnessed several heated arguments between them."

Faith's gaze shot between Aiden and Chase. "I'm confused. What difference does it make if Hillary inherited money from her grandparents?"

"Silas may want to get his hands on it," Aiden said. "If Hillary dies, Anna would inherit the money."

Beside him, Faith inhaled sharply. "That's why he tried to kidnap her from the grocery store."

Chase kept quiet. He didn't want to scare Faith unnecessarily, and there was no proof of the dark suspicions running through his head. Faith opened her mouth to say something else but was cut off by her cell phone. She glanced at the screen. "I'm sorry. I need to take this. My parents are still on vacation, and this is their next-door neighbor."

She rose from her chair and slipped out of the office. Chase watched her through the glass wall. Nearby, Holly was holding Anna, rocking the little girl gently.

People did horrible things, but it was beyond comprehension to harm an innocent child for money. Yet that might be exactly what was happening here. While Chase didn't want to scare Faith, he had no compunction about voicing his theory to Aiden. "It's unlikely a judge would grant Silas custody of Anna, given his criminal background. He's not interested in becoming her guardian. He needs her gone."

Aiden heaved a sigh. "I agree with you. Silas has deadly intentions toward that little girl. Getting rid of her is the only way he'll get the money."

Chase kept Faith in eyesight but directed his question toward Aiden. "Have you interviewed Silas?"

"We tried." Aiden glowered. "He's missing. Silas hasn't been seen since the night Hillary disappeared. He doesn't have a permanent residence, usually bunks with a rotating list of friends. He also doesn't own a car." He flipped to a few more photographs on the tablet. "These are stills taken from the surveillance video of the grocery store parking lot. The attacker used a silver truck as a getaway vehicle. It's the same make and model as Hillary's vehicle."

"He's using her car." Chase blew out a breath. "Wow."

"I've got every officer in the state looking for Silas and this vehicle. We're going to find him."

Chase didn't doubt his boss's determination or investigative skills, but if they were right about Silas, the man had nothing to lose. He would try to hurt Anna again, and he'd tried to eliminate Faith as a potential witness to his sister's murder. They needed to get him off the streets. Immediately.

Faith hurried back into the office, panic stamped on her pretty features. Chase shot to his feet. "What is it?"

"It's my parents' house. A water pipe burst and it's

flooding." She grabbed her purse from the chair. "We have to go."

"Leave the baby with Holly and me," Aiden said quickly. He shot Chase a concerned look. The message was loud and clear: be careful.

Chase nodded, his own mind already whirling with possibilities as he followed Faith out of the office. The burst pipe could be a coincidence. Or Hillary's killer could have broken into the house and busted the pipe, knowing Faith would be called over to check things out.

Were they walking into a trap?

NINE

Faith gripped the keys to her parents' house tight in her hand. Dark clouds had erased the morning's blue sky, as the bad weather predicted by the forecasters came to fruition. A chill raced down her spine. Ahead of her, Chase had palmed his weapon. A precautionary move, but one that reinforced the constant danger surrounding them. He'd explained the possibility that they'd been lured to her parents' house by the killer. Faith was grateful Holly and Aiden had kept Anna at the police station. The baby would be safe there.

Chase reached behind him with one hand. "Give me the keys, Faith."

She did as he requested. His heavy jacket accented his broad shoulders and blocked her view of the door. There was no way to miss the river of water running down the cement steps into the yard. The neighbor had been right. Something in the house was leaking.

Chase opened the door and more water poured out of the house. Faith gasped. She jumped out of the way. A pipe under the sink in the mudroom was flinging cold water all over the tile floor. She hurried to shut off the main valve located just inside the back door. "What a mess."

"The water didn't get too high, thankfully. There's no water damage on the walls." Chase kept his weapon in his hand. "Stay here and let me clear the rest of the house. Then we can mop the floor."

Faith nodded. She chewed on her fingernail as he disappeared around the corner. The wind kicked up, rustling her hair and seeping in the collar of her jacket. The sense of being watched swept over her.

She spun. A squirrel jumped from the oak tree onto the bird feeder. She let out the breath she was holding and forced her muscles to relax. Things were bad enough without jumping at her own shadow. Chase's footsteps preceded him back into the mudroom. His weapon was holstered. "There's no one here."

"Well, that's something to be grateful for." Faith took another deep breath and forced her muscles to relax. She assessed the water damage. It wasn't as bad as she'd originally thought. "You're right. The water didn't get high enough to damage the walls. Mom and Dad were fortunate. They're coming home Christmas Eve from their trip, so it's not urgent we fix this today. I'll call a plumber and we'll arrange for him to come by tomorrow."

For the next hour, Faith and Chase cleaned the mudroom. He kept her laughing with bad jokes and funny stories, which made the chore fun. He had a way of doing that. Making everything seem easier.

By the time they made it back into the truck, heading toward town to pick up Anna, the weather had grown worse. The windshield wipers worked overtime to handle the sleet painting the glass. Ice coated the trees as the temperature dropped by the second.

Chase cranked the heater to full blast and switched on the defroster to clear the fog blocking their view of the road. "Looks like you won't have to worry about missing the Christmas Fair after all. With this weather, they'll have to cancel it."

She nodded absently. Now that the immediate crisis with the broken pipe was over, Faith's mind turned to the deadly attacks and Hillary's murder. She was brokenhearted over the young woman's death. And poor little Anna. To have lost her mother at such a tender age... It was too painful to think about. Faith shoved her emotions to the side. They wouldn't help her. Since leaving Aiden's office, there was one nagging thought that'd plagued her.

"Chase, if Hillary's brother murdered her, why did he do it in Cutler? They both lived in Austin. Wouldn't it have been simpler to kill her there?"

His hands tightened on the steering wheel. "Yes, but Silas may have thought killing Hillary in a small town would work to his benefit. There's a common misconception that cases won't be taken as seriously or that the police are sloppy." He was quiet for a long moment. "Although you bring up a good point. Nothing in his criminal record indicates he has the foresight to plan a complicated murder. He's more the type to kill someone in the spur of the moment."

Some of the tension in Faith's shoulder loosened. She wasn't a police officer, and while Chase had never demeaned her intelligence, it made her slightly nervous to challenge Aiden's theory of the case. He was a good man, one who took pride in his job and did it well.

She removed a cloth from the glove box before swiping at the passenger-side window. The defroster was having a hard time keeping up with the abnormal Texas weather. Headlights shimmered behind them, but the driver appeared to be a safe distance away. Trees towered above them on the left. The right-hand side dipped down toward a small valley.

"I keep thinking about the way Dr. Whitcomb was looking at Anna." Faith handed Chase the cloth and he swiped at his own window. "I know he has an alibi, but..." She bit her lip. "Is it possible he faked it? If Robert is Anna's father, then he could be behind these attacks."

Chase glanced in the rearview mirror. "First, we can't jump to conclusions. We don't know if Robert is Anna's father. Second, faking an alibi isn't easy to do. It's not impossible, but in my experience, most criminals don't bother."

"I don't think the man who killed Hillary and attacked me is like most criminals."

He grimaced. "Good point."

A flash of silver caught Faith's eye as they passed an offshoot road. She turned in her seat just as the truck's tires skid across the asphalt. Her heart leapt to her throat.

Black ice.

Faith screamed as the vehicle went into a spin. Headlights flashed across her vision moments before the car behind them slammed into the truck. Glass shattered, raining down onto her clothes and hair. The momentum of the collision pushed them over the edge of the road. Everything moved in slow motion as Faith braced for what was coming next. Her gaze locked on Chase. His hands gripped the wheel, determination etched on his features, as he desperately tried to stop the inevitable.

The truck tumbled over the incline. Metal screeched. Faith's seat belt gripped her shoulder with a bruising force. The world blurred brown and green as the truck flipped. Inside her head, Faith was screaming, but there wasn't enough air in her lungs for the sound to carry past her lips. Black spots danced in front of her vision.

They came to a shuddering stop in an upright position. Faith gulped in air, belatedly realizing she'd been holding her breath. The scent of pine and earth surrounded her. Everything was eerily quiet after the deafening noise of the crash. Her air bag hadn't deployed since all the impact had been on the side or the rear. Faith blinked, struggling to kick her brain into motion. "Chase?"

"I'm okay." A hand landed on her shoulder. "Don't move, Faith. You're hurt."

She ignored his direction and raised trembling fingers to her temple. Warm liquid coated her skin, and when she pulled her hand away, she was shocked to discover blood on her palm. Pain rippled out from her stitches. "I don't think it's serious. My wound reopened."

While Chase called in the accident to dispatch, she went through a mental rundown of her body, moving her legs and arms to make sure nothing was broken. Other than the bleeding head wound, she was fine. After he hung up, she reassured him. "I'm okay."

"Still, it's better to stay put until the medics arrive. They're on the way." Chase released his seat belt, and the movement caused glass to fall from his hair. He had a cut along one cheek but otherwise appeared unharmed to Faith's untrained eye. He retrieved an emergency blanket from underneath his seat and covered her with it. Then he pressed gauze to her bleeding head wound. "Hold this here. I'm going to check on the driver of the other vehicle. I'll be right back."

As a police officer, it was his duty to provide first aid. Faith wasn't badly injured, and she prayed the people in the other vehicle weren't either. Still, a bolt of fear jolted through her. She trembled. The broken windows allowed cold and sleet to seep into the truck's cab. Something niggled her, but Faith couldn't get her brain to operate correctly. Her thoughts felt muddled. She grabbed Chase's arm before he could back away from her. "Please be careful."

"I will." He kissed her forehead.

The move was tender and sweet and inexplicably brought tears to her eyes. She blinked them back. By the time her vision cleared, Chase was halfway up the steep incline, headed for the road. He held a first aid kit in one hand.

Something flashed in the trees. Another vehicle had arrived at the scene of the accident. Faith's chest clenched as she realized it was a silver truck. Suddenly, the memory trying to work its way into her consciousness burst through. They'd passed the same truck waiting on an offshoot road. Chase's fears about the broken pipe at her parents' house roared back to life as Faith realized he'd been right all along. They'd walked into a trap.

CHRISTMAS THREAT

The ice on the road wasn't because of the weather. It'd been planted.

"Chase!" Faith screamed his name just as the sound of a gunshot ripped through the air.

She was helpless to do anything as her best friend crumpled to the ground.

God, no! Not Chase!

She popped open the glove box, desperately fumbling for some kind of weapon. She refused to even consider it might be too late to protect him. Tears ran down her cheeks.

The dark-clad figure turned toward the truck. His arm rose.

A surge of survival instinct pushed away her terror for Chase as Faith pressed on the button to release her seat belt. Something whizzed past her ear and thudded into the door panel.

A bullet.

Faith dropped to the floor board. Her breath came short and fast.

She was trapped.

TEN

Gunshots.

Chase struggled against the icy slope and slid another few inches down the incline. Frigid water seeped through his jeans. The sleet had turned to a drizzle, but the damage was already done. The entire side of the hill was covered in ice. Faith's warning scream had caused Chase to lose his footing. It'd also saved his life.

His foot lodged in a tree root, blessedly providing him traction. His right shoulder screamed in pain—dislocated?—and his hip ached. But he barely acknowledged the pain. The shooter, at the road's edge, was aiming for Faith. Chase had to stop him.

He struggled to unholster his weapon, his fingers fumbling with the button holding the weapon securely in place. His dominant hand was utterly useless, putting him at a distinct disadvantage. The shooter was wearing black clothing and a ski mask. An engine fired up, and the vehicle Chase had collided with earlier sped off. Better. The last thing he needed was another civilian in the shooter's sights. This criminal was intent on not leaving witnesses.

Another shot exploded, followed by the ping of metal as it collided with Chase's truck. Terror for Faith lodged itself in Chase's heart. He blocked it out. He was no good to her if his mind was muddled by emotion. He re-doubled his efforts to free his weapon. Using his right hand made him want to scream. Where was his backup? Why was it taking so long?

Please, God, I could use your help here.

Grass crunched as the man in black stepped off the asphalt and headed toward the damaged vehicle at the bottom of the incline. Toward Faith. Chase's blood ran piping hot as his vision grew hazy with rage. There was no time to arm himself. "Police! Drop your weapon!"

The man whirled, gun raised. Bullets thudded into the tree. Chase expected the move—shouting at the criminal drew attention away from Faith—and rolled. Pain erupted through his entire chest as his hurt arm protested the movement. His gun flung free from the holster. It slid across an ice patch on the incline, landing a short distance away. Chase threw himself at it. He lifted the weapon awkwardly in his left hand, aimed, and fired.

The shot went wide. The gunman returned fire and Chase was forced to roll again. Dirt and ice water clung to his clothes. The pain from his arm was blinding. White-hot agony. Still, he clung to his weapon.

He skidded to a stop behind a large pine and used it as cover. Sucking in a deep breath, he gritted his teeth and pitched to an upright position. The gunman hadn't moved any closer to the truck. Chase intended to keep it that way. He took aim and fired, but once again, the shot went wide.

The sound of wailing sirens echoed through the air. The police were closing in. The gunman must've heard them, too, because he bolted for his vehicle. A silver truck. Chase balanced against the tree and stood. He peered through the brush to glimpse the license plate, but it was no use. The truck's engine roared as it peeled away.

There was no way to stop him. The approaching sirens were still too far away. Chase's gaze shot to his own truck sitting at the bottom of the incline. His heart stuttered as the full realization of what'd transpired crashed down on him. The gunman had gotten off several rounds before Chase had intervened. Was Faith hit?

Had she been killed?

The thought sliced through the last shred of self-control he had. Abandoning any sense of reason, or the threat of sliding on more ice, Chase recklessly ran for his vehicle. "Faith!"

The passenger-side door flung open. Faith emerged. Her hair was bloody from the wound on her scalp. Mascara and tear tracks ran down her face. Her clothes were stained, wrinkled, and sparkling with broken glass.

Chase had never seen anything more beautiful in his life.

Faith raced for him, her body colliding with his as she wrapped her arms around him. Pain from his arm ricocheted through his core, but he ignored it. Chase wrapped his good arm around her waist, hauling her against his body. Every inch of him was aware of her. He buried his face in her hair. The scent of her perfume, light and cinnamony, surrounded him. He released a shuddering breath.

She pulled back far enough to cup his face in between her chilled hands. Faith locked gazes with him, her gorgeous brown eyes filling with fresh tears. "I thought you were dead."

Before he could say likewise, she pitched forward and kissed him.

The world stopped.

Chase had envisioned and daydreamed what it would be like to kiss Faith a thousand times. Nothing could prepare him for the real thing. Her lips were soft but carried passion unlike he'd ever experienced. His knees nearly buckled under the swell of emotion. Her fingers sank into the hair along the nape of his neck and Chase deepened the kiss, pulling Faith even closer. Her petite form fit in his arms as if they'd been made for each other. Kissing her...it was everything. He didn't want it to end.

The wail of sirens cut through the haze of his passion. Faith pulled back, breathless. Their gazes locked and held. Something flickered in the depth of her eyes.

Regret.

Chase's heart sank to his dirty boots as reality sent him crashing back to earth. Faith had initiated the kiss, and he was certain it meant something to her, but that didn't change the circumstances. She was still in love with her late husband. Maybe she would always be.

A cold chill that had nothing to do with the drizzle or the pain from his arm rippled through his body. He was a fool heading straight into a heartbreak, and if Chase wasn't careful, he was going to lose his best friend. Faith's gaze skittered away from his and her cheeks flushed. Proof of her embarrassment. Chase released her just as a police car pulled up. He struggled to find something to say, anything to let her know things hadn't changed between them, but the words wouldn't come.

How could they? Nothing was ever going to be the same again.

ELEVEN

Hours later, Chase exited the exam room of the ER. His dislocated shoulder had been reset and his arm was in a sling. He was under strict orders from the doctor to rest, but with Faith's attacker still out there, recuperation wasn't his first priority. Keeping her and Anna safe was.

Not that he was doing a good job of it. Chase had worked hard to distance himself from the reckless teenager he used to be, but this case was tearing at all those old wounds. He felt like a failure. Coupled with anxiety over kissing Faith and the pain from his injuries, he was in a foul mood. He shoved the door leading to the waiting room with more force than necessary and marched over the threshold.

David Carpenter, Chase's friend and a fellow officer with the Cutler Police Department, was waiting with Faith in the corner of the room. His six-foot-tall frame was encased in a bulletproof vest that widened his bulky frame. In one hand, he held a cup of coffee. Two others—one for Faith and perhaps Chase?—rested on a nearby table. David grinned. "Took you long enough, McKenzie. I was beginning to think they'd never set you loose."

"You and me both."

"How bad is your arm?" Faith rose from a chair. Her head wound had been restitched, but blood still matted the strands of her hair. She was pale, her features pinched.

Chase wanted to gather her into his arms and kiss that worry from her beautiful face, but didn't dare. He'd learned a long time ago to smother his feelings for Faith behind a wall of pretense. So instead of touching her, he forced the corners of his mouth into an easy smile. "Dislocated, but the doctor reset it and I get to wear this sexy sling for a few weeks. I'm hoping it'll earn me another batch of your brownies."

The comment had the desired effect. Faith rolled her eyes. "For heaven's sake. Brownies aren't the answer to everything."

"Maybe not." He winked. "But it doesn't hurt to have them either."

She laughed. "I can't argue with you there." Faith retrieved one of the takeaway cups and handed it to him. "Coffee."

"Thanks." He turned to David. "What's the update?"

David hooked his thumbs into his belt loops. "The shooter got away. Crime scene techs are working the scene now, and I've had your truck towed to the evidence shed, but so far, we've got nothing new."

"What about the civilian in the other vehicle? Is she okay?"

"Yes. She drove straight to the police station after leaving the scene of the accident. The chief interviewed her, but all she remembers is seeing a man dressed in black holding a gun." David frowned. "From what we've been able to piece together, the shooter saw y'all to go to the Hicks' house. Then he spread water on the road to create black ice and lay in wait for you nearby. The woman driving the sedan was an innocent bystander."

Faith wrapped her arms around herself. "It's a miracle no one was killed."

Chase nodded as a wave of fresh anger washed through him. The black ice on the road had been a desperate and reckless move. It was clear this criminal didn't care how many people he put in danger. And Chase didn't want to even think about what could've happened if the baby had been in the truck with them at the time of the accident. His hand tightened around the takeaway coffee mug and it crumbled under the force of his grip.

David pulled a set of keys from his pocket. "I'll drive y'all home. The chief and Holly will meet us there with the baby." He clapped Chase on the back. "Glad you're okay, man. We've got everyone in the department working this case. We'll catch him."

"Appreciate it, David." Chase didn't doubt the work ethic of his department. They would move heaven and earth to catch the criminal responsible. But how long would it take? And how many more dangerous situations would Faith and Anna be put in?

David left the waiting room, and Chase tossed his creased coffee mug into a nearby trash can. A cold blast of air rippled across his face as the sliding doors swished open. Dr. Robert Whitcomb strolled in. He carried a briefcase in one hand and an insulated lunch sack in the other. His gaze landed on Faith, and he beelined straight for her, a determined expression etched on his face.

Chase stepped between them. "Doctor Whitcomb, is there something you need?"

His tone came out harsher than he intended, but it couldn't be helped. Chase hadn't been able to stop thinking about Faith's comments in the car on the way to her parents' house. Robert had looked strangely at Anna during their first visit to the hospital. Was the man hiding something? Was he Anna's father?

Had he killed Hillary?

Robert came to a halt. He blinked in surprise. "I received a phone call from the doctor on duty. He said Faith's wound had been reopened after she was involved in a car accident. I want to check on her."

"That's kind of you." Faith placed a reassuring hand on Chase's arm. "I'm a bit worse for the wear, but the doctor said I'll be fine in a few days."

"This is connected to Hillary's murder, isn't it? I've heard the rumors around town about the baby found in your barn. The police questioned me the other day. Why would anyone want to hurt Hillary or her baby?"

"We're trying to figure that out." Chase forced his muscles to relax. "It's my understanding you and Hillary broke up shortly before she moved out of town. Did you know she'd had a baby?"

Robert sighed. "Yes. We didn't speak often after she moved to Austin, but we occasionally texted each other."

"Who is Anna's father?"

"I don't know. That's the reason Hillary and I broke up. She had fallen in love with someone else but refused to say who." Sadness bracketed the sides of his mouth. "I loved her. I'm not ashamed to admit that, and it broke my heart when she ended our relationship. Secretly, I think a part of me was hoping the new relationship would fall apart, and she'd come back to me." Tears filmed his eyes. "Obviously, that won't happen now."

Either Robert was truly distraught over Hillary's death or he was an excellent actor. Still, there were lingering questions. Chase remembered the strange way the doctor had looked at the baby. Faith must've been thinking the same thing because she said, "You recognized Anna when we brought her into the hospital a couple of days ago. Why didn't you say anything?"

Robert shifted his lunchbox to the same hand with his briefcase and then pinched the bridge of his nose. "I didn't recognize Anna. At least...not with certainty. Hillary had sent me a few pictures, and there was a resemblance, but I thought it was my imagination." He dropped his hand. "I'm sorry. I should've voiced my suspicions, but there was no reason to believe Hillary and Anna were in Cutler. They'd moved to Austin, remember?"

His explanation seemed reasonable. And Dr. Whitcomb had an alibi for the night of the grocery store attack. He was working at the hospital. Chase had questioned the nursing staff while waiting for his arm to be examined. Several had confirmed Robert arrived hours before the attack and left long after. There was no way he was responsible.

"What do you know about the relationship between Hillary and her brother?" Chase asked.

Robert's expression darkened. "It wasn't good. Silas was

a constant source of trouble. Hillary bailed him out of jail more than once and gave him money periodically. He took advantage of her." The doctor's gaze darted around the waiting room, as if to make sure no one was listening to their conversation. Then he settled his attention back on Chase. "If you want my opinion, I'd take a good hard look at Silas. I never saw him do anything violent toward Hillary, but the man has a temper when he's using drugs or alcohol. Hillary used to tell me about their fights, and what she described sounded unhealthy at best, abusive at worst."

"Thank you for the information." Beyond the glass window, Chase caught sight of David's cruiser pulling up to the doors. He placed a hand on the small of Faith's back. "That's our ride. If you think of anything else, Dr. Whitcomb, please contact the police department."

"I will." He shook Chase's outstretched hand and then Faith's before turning to leave. Something dropped out of his jacket pocket onto the tile floor.

A black ski mask.

TWELVE

Faith gently pushed against the carpet with her feet to keep the rocking chair in motion. Anna's bright blue eyes were latched onto her face, even as her mouth worked the bottle. She smelled like baby soap. A warm bath had put color in her cheeks, the glow from the lamp on the end table caressing the curves of the baby's face. One tiny hand clung to Faith's pinky finger.

Anna was so small...so vulnerable. A love unlike anything Faith had ever experienced lodged inside her heart. It'd been growing for days, from the first moment she touched the baby in the barn, and denying it wasn't possible anymore. She'd do anything for Anna. Anything. Including risk her own life to protect her, if it came to it. Faith prayed it wouldn't.

Who had killed Hillary? They were no closer to figuring that out than they'd been hours ago. The black ski mask that'd fallen out of Dr. Whitcomb's jacket didn't prove his involvement. It was winter and the temperatures were cold enough for snow. Not to mention, he had an alibi for at least one of the attacks. Still…it made Faith nervous.

Silas, Hillary's brother, was still missing as well. It was horrifying to think he might have murdered his own sister and attempted to kidnap his niece, but Faith wouldn't dismiss the possibility. If Hillary and Anna were both dead, Silas stood to inherit a large sum of money. Greed could twist people into doing evil things.

But what about the mystery man Hillary had been dating? Who was Anna's father? The police in Austin had interviewed friends, coworkers, and neighbors, but no one had seen Hillary with a man. Nor had she ever talked about the baby's dad. It was a strange set of circumstances, and nothing about it sat right.

Anna's fingers relaxed against Faith's pinky. The baby's eyes were drifting shut, now that her belly was full. Faith waited for her to take a few last sucks from the bottle before gently removing it from Anna's mouth. She brushed a kiss across her forehead. "Sleep, little one."

Her heart swelled when Anna released a sigh of contentment. Faith tried to remind herself that the baby wasn't hers to keep, but the mental gymnastics weren't working. Much like they hadn't with Chase. The memory of the kiss they'd shared hours ago seemed imprinted on her lips.

Chase appeared at the base of the stairs. He wore a pair of beat-up blue jeans and a soft gray T-shirt that molded to every inch of his muscular chest. His feet were bare. The sling holding his injured arm should've made him appear weaker, but had the opposite effect. To Faith, it was a symbol of his bravery. He'd nearly died today while protecting her.

Chase separated the blinds with one finger and peeked out into the night. His hair was still damp from his shower. He scanned the yard. Faith's muscles instinctively tightened. "Is something wrong?"

"No." He dropped his hand. "I'm just being cautious. David is parked nearby and will make patrols on the property. We'll reassess the situation in the morning, but for tonight, there's no reason to worry. The house is secure."

It was something to be grateful for. They could all use a good night's rest after the past several days. Faith lowered a sleeping Anna to the playpen and then covered the baby with a fleece blanket. Chase sidled up next to her, close enough to tease her senses with the warmth of his body and the scent of his aftershave. A smile played on his lips. "She looks so peaceful. I wonder what she dreams about."

"Soft hugs and tender touches, I hope." Faith kept her voice lowered to a whisper out of habit more than a fear of waking the baby. Anna slept through almost everything. "We have a few hours till the next feeding and I could use your help with something."

"What?"

She gestured to the plastic tubs on the other side of the room. "Holly helped me bring down the decorations from the attic and set up the Christmas tree. I thought we could decorate." Faith bit her lip, a sudden wave of nervousness washing over her. "If your shoulder hurts, you don't have to do anything. Or if you're too tired, we can skip it."

"No. I'd like to help." His gaze met hers, confusion

creasing his brow. "I'm just surprised. You didn't want to decorate a tree last year."

"Not since Mitch died. I know." She took his hand and gently tugged him across the room. Faith opened a tub. Neatly packed string lights rested next to a pile of tinsel. "But I've been thinking a lot of the last few days. You know, when I wasn't busy running for my life or making brownies."

That last comment earned her half a smile. Chase removed the lights and sat down on a dining room chair to test the bulbs by plugging them into the socket. The bright colors blinked to life. "These work." He unraveled them and started draping them on the tree branches. "Don't stop talking. I'm listening."

Nerves once again jittered her insides. It didn't make sense. She'd faced near-death experiences with less panic. But sharing her thoughts with Chase, after their spontaneous and passionate kiss earlier today, felt dangerous. Like she was voicing something that couldn't be taken back.

Then again, boundaries had already been broken. The unspoken attraction humming between them wasn't going away. Chase, to his credit, had attempted to keep things normal. But eventually they had to talk about it. In her mind, the sooner, the better. Time would only make it more awkward.

"I've been stuck in a holding pattern since Mitch's death. There were so many things I wanted for my life. Children, for example." She glanced at the baby, sleeping sweetly in her playpen. "Anna's arrival forced me to realize that maybe those things aren't as out of reach as I thought."

Chase paused. "You're thinking of adopting her?"

"I can't bear the thought of letting her go, so...yes." Faith swallowed hard. "I know it won't be easy—"

"Nothing good worth having ever is." He placed a hand over hers. A current of warmth coursed up Faith's arm, and when she lifted her gaze to meet his, the admiration shining from his eyes stole her breath. "You're going to make an amazing mom, Faith, and if you want to adopt Anna, I'll do everything I can to help you."

She was at a loss for words. How could she have been so blind? These feelings she'd been developing for Chase weren't one-sided after all. His love for her was as clear as a summer's day. Her heart thundered so loud, Faith was certain he could hear it. She took a step toward him. One more and she'd be in his arms. The desire to kiss him again overwhelmed her, but the wary look in Chase's expression stopped her. Faith froze.

Was she wrong about his feelings?

Chase's cell phone chimed with an incoming message. He dropped Faith's hand, the swiftness of his movements catching her off guard. She wrapped her arms around herself. Heat crept into her cheeks as the sense of foolishness swept over her. Heavens, she might have seriously embarrassed herself. First with that kiss and now by misinterpreting Chase's offer to help with Anna. Faith wanted the floor to swallow her whole.

The last few days had been fraught with emotions. It was making her see things that weren't there.

Chase frowned as he read the text message. "David says your neighbor, Tom Bradley, is headed up the drive. Were you expecting him?"

Clinging to the distraction like it was a lifeline, Faith

shook her head. "Not at all. But maybe he thought of something else pertaining to Hillary and the case."

Faith followed Chase to the front door. Tom, bundled in a thick wool coat and gloves, hurried from his SUV up the walkway. He carried a basket in his hands. A sliver of fear ran down Faith's spine, but she shook it off. There was no reason to be afraid of Tom.

She waited until he reached the bottom porch step and then unlocked and opened the front door. A blast of frigid air washed over her cheeks. "Tom, what a pleasant surprise. Please come in."

"Sorry, I can't stay." He thrust the basket in her direction. "My wife asked me to drop this off. I've got four more to deliver before it gets dark and the icy rain comes back."

Faith took the gift. Cookies, hot chocolate, scones, and other goodies were visible through the clear cellophane wrapper covering the outside. A handwritten card dangled from the ribbon at the top. It read Merry Christmas. Marsha sent over a gift basket every year.

Tom ran a gloved hand over his beard. "The sweets are homemade. Marsha made them with the kids this afternoon."

"That's so kind. Thank you."

He waved off her appreciation. "It's the least we could do after all the trouble you've been going through recently. It's good you have extra protection from the police. I heard about the car accident y'all were in this morning. Glad to see you're all right."

Faith wasn't surprised by that. Cutler was a small town and news traveled fast.

Tom's gaze drifted toward Chase standing guard nearby. "Is there any progress on the case?"

"Every officer in the department is actively working on it." Chase was angled behind the door so his sling wasn't visible, but his muscles were tense. Faith had the sense he was prepared to spring into a protective mode should the need arise. Clearly, she wasn't the only one feeling on edge. "We're determined to get to the truth."

Tom shook his head. "I keep thinking about Hillary. I can't get over the fact that she's dead. It's surreal."

Some emotion buried in his voice caught Faith's attention. She'd heard rumors around town that Tom had a wandering eye, but she'd never put any stock in it. Gossip always bothered her. But the fact that Hillary had kept the identity of her father's child secret niggled her. Why would she do that unless there was a very good reason? Faith gripped the door handle. "How close were you and Hillary?"

Tom's gaze narrowed at the question. "We weren't close at all. She was a sweet woman, that's all."

Beside Faith, Chase stiffened. He'd obviously caught on to what she was alluding to. Not surprising in the least. The man had always been able to follow her chain of thought—with one exception. Her feelings about him.

Chase stepped closer to Faith, his chest pressing against her back. "We've been told she was having a secret relationship. You wouldn't know anything about that, would you? Did Hillary ever mention dating someone other than Dr. Whitcomb?"

"Not to me." Tom's tone was light. "Like I said, we

weren't close. I'll ask my wife though. You know women. They chatter sometimes."

The frosty air was numbing her fingers. Faith gestured for Tom to come inside, hoping they could wheedle a few more minutes of his time. It might help determine if there was anything more than a professional relationship between him and Hillary. "Would you like a cup of coffee? Or tea?"

"No, thank you." He offered her a smile. "Like I said, I've got four more baskets to deliver before the icy rain starts back up again. I'd better get a move on." Tom bounded down the porch steps. "Y'all have a good night."

"You too." Faith waved and then shut the front door. She watched Tom climb into his SUV and drive away. "Well, that was interesting. Is it just me, or did Tom act as if he had something to hide?"

"Could be." Chase shrugged. "Then again, gossip and rumors could be coloring our impressions. I've heard Tom has cheated on his wife a time or two, but I don't know how valid that information is. And even if it's true, that doesn't mean he had a secret relationship with Hillary. We have to be careful and let the evidence lead us, otherwise we'll head in the wrong direction."

Faith nodded, guilt pricking her. Chase was right. They had no evidence that Hillary and Tom were romantically involved. Once again, he seemed to follow the chain of her thoughts because he said, "I'll ask Aiden to re-interview Hillary's friends, specifically asking them about her relationship with the Bradleys. Maybe there's more to this than we know at the moment."

She let out a breath she was holding. "Thank you, Chase." Faith picked up the gift basket from the table next to the door. "Well, you're in for a real treat. Marsha's hot chocolate is homemade. Some kind of special blend of light and dark cocoa. It's delicious. Want a cup?"

"Sure." Faith started for the kitchen, but Chase stopped her with a hand on her arm. His touch was warm and firm. "Wait. Before we have hot chocolate, maybe we should talk. Anna will wake up soon for her bottle and this isn't something we can put off."

Her heart skipped a beat. She had a sinking feeling Chase wanted to discuss that second near-kiss from a few minutes ago. But Faith's emotions were so raw and exposed, she didn't trust herself to handle his rejection with grace.

"It's okay, Chase. I already know what you're going to say. We don't need to talk about it."

Faith shook off his hand and headed for the kitchen. Relief weakened her knees when the swinging door closed behind her. Hot tears pressed against her eyes. Silly, foolish tears. What on earth was she so upset about? She'd known all along Chase didn't see her romantically.

She undid the ribbon on the gift basket. The scents of chocolate and vanilla wafted up. Faith breathed them in, letting the comforting smells soothe her hurt feelings. From inside the living room, Chase's ringtone sang out, followed by the low murmur of his voice.

His footsteps preceded him into the kitchen. Faith sucked in a breath before turning to face him. Her muscles stiffened at the look on his face. "What is it?"

Chase lifted his cell phone. "Aiden called. They've found Silas."

THIRTEEN

Two hours later, Chase stood with Aiden outside the interrogation room. Through the clear glass walls of the police chief's office, Faith was visible. She was feeding Anna a bottle. Her dark hair was pulled into a low ponytail and she seemed to be singing a tune. The side door to the office opened and Holly entered, bearing cups of coffee and a takeaway bag from the local bakery down the street.

Chase and Faith hadn't discussed their kiss or the feelings sparking between them. He wanted to. Desperately. But the case had to take precedence. Faith and Anna's safety depended on it.

"One of my officers responded to a tip that Silas was camping in the local state park." Aiden's words cut through Chase's thoughts and brought his attention back to the matter at hand. "He located him on a rarely used trail. Silas had Hillary's truck with him."

"What does he have to say about his sister's murder?"

"He claims to not have known until we told him." Aiden frowned. "Truth be told, I'm tempted to believe him.

Silas broke down when I informed him of Hillary's death. But when I asked why he had her truck, he refused to say."

"This isn't his first run-in with the law." Chase eyed the man sitting in the interrogation room through the small window next to the door. Silas wore a gray T-shirt and faded jeans. His tennis shoes had seen better days, and his hair was disheveled. Silas's eyes were swollen and red from crying. Real tears? Like Aiden, Chase wanted to believe so, but he'd seen too many criminals who could fake their emotional reaction. "I'm sure Silas is afraid we're looking to pin his sister's murder on him."

"Or something else. We didn't locate any drugs in the truck or his campsite, nor were there any alcohol bottles. There was a chip from AA though. One month sober."

AA was Alcoholics Anonymous, an organization that aided people with addiction. Chase rocked back on his heels. The chip, given to Silas for staying sober for one month, didn't necessarily mean anything. It could be old. "Even if Silas is sober, it doesn't mean he didn't steal his sister's truck or kill her."

"Agreed, but right now, we don't have any proof he's done anything wrong. Officially, Silas isn't under arrest. He's at the station voluntarily. I can't hold him for trespassing on state property, because he'd paid to rent the campsite. I don't have proof he stole his sister's vehicle either. And there's nothing concrete linking him to the murder." Aiden ran a hand through his hair. "Crime scene technicians are combing Hillary's truck for evidence, but so far, they haven't come up with anything. I was giving Silas some time to think things over before attempting to question him again."

Frustration bit at Chase. He glanced at Faith and Anna before focusing back on the man in the interrogation room. "Let me talk to him."

Aiden narrowed his gaze. "Can you maintain your cool?"

"Absolutely." Chase straightened to his full height. "No one wants this case solved more than I do, and the evidence has to be rock solid. I don't want to catch the murderer, only to have him walk free because of a technicality. I'll do it by the book. You have my word."

His boss studied his face for a long moment and then nodded. Chase hurried into the break room and grabbed a few waters, along with a snack for Silas. They hadn't had any luck treating him like a criminal. Changing tactics and acknowledging he was a grieving brother might convince Silas to tell what he knew.

Chase entered the interrogation room and set the drinks down on the table. "Mr. Evans, my name is Detective Chase McKenzie. I'd like to ask you a few questions, if that's all right." He pushed the food across the table. "Bought you something to eat and drink. It's well past dinnertime, and I figured you might be hungry. If you want something else, let me know and we'll make arrangements."

Silas barely glanced at the food. "I couldn't think of eating." He ran a shaky hand through his mussed hair, making the dark strands stand up on end. "Am I under arrest?"

"No, sir. As Police Chief James explained earlier, we're investigating Hillary's murder." Chase held his gaze. "And we need your help to do it. The sooner you answer my questions, the faster we can get justice for your sister. All I'm interested in is the truth."

"The truth?"

He held the other man's gaze. "Yes."

Silas nodded his head in agreement. Chase went through the procedural paperwork necessary to question Hillary's brother, including advising him of his Miranda rights. Everything by the book, as he'd promised Aiden. He wanted whatever Silas said to be admissible in court.

Chase set aside the paperwork but kept his pen handy to take notes. "When was the last time you saw Hillary?"

"A few days ago. On Thursday evening."

The night Hillary went missing. She was murdered early Friday morning. Chase's gut tightened. That placed the victim with her brother hours before her death. Was Silas aware of that? Maybe not. Aiden had told him of Hillary's murder but probably didn't go into details. Chase stole a quick glance at the camera mounted on the wall. Aiden was observing the interview in an adjacent room that housed their recording equipment.

Silas opened a bottle of water and took a swig. He grimaced as though the clear liquid was distasteful. "Hillary came to my campsite with Anna…" His eyes widened. "The police chief told me Anna is okay. He was telling the truth about that, wasn't he?"

The concern etched across Silas's face seemed genuine, but Chase didn't put much stock in it. Criminals, especially experienced ones, knew how to lie. "Anna's unharmed and being kept someplace safe."

Silas's shoulders relaxed. "Good. Good." He nodded. "Okay, where was I? Oh yeah, Hillary came to my campsite with Anna. I'd sent my sister an email the week before explaining to her I was sober, attending AA meetings, and had a sponsor."

His expression grew distant as he stared at the opposite wall, as if visualizing a memory. "My relationship with Hillary hasn't been good in the last few years. My drinking was a big part of that." He focused back on Chase. "I reached out via email because I wanted to make amends for my past behavior."

"And did you?"

Silas nodded. "Hillary…" His voice thickened and a thin film of tears shone in his eyes. "Hillary said she was proud of me. We spent a long time talking. Most of the afternoon, in fact. Then Hillary asked me to drive her into town and drop her off. She wanted to meet with someone but didn't say who."

"What time was this?"

"Around eight."

Chase's heart rate picked up speed. That was less than twelve hours before she was murdered. Was Silas telling the truth about dropping his sister off in town, or was he trying to cover his tracks? Chase was suspicious but kept his tone and expression neutral. "You didn't think it was strange that Hillary asked you to drop her off in town? Why didn't she simply drive herself?"

Silas took another swig of water and wiped his mouth with the back of his hand. "Her truck was having carburetor problems. I was a mechanic before drinking took over my life. While she was running her errands, I was going to repair her truck. She was going to catch a ride with a friend back to my campsite."

"Weren't you worried when Hillary never came back for her truck?"

Silas tore at the label on the water bottle. "No. In hindsight, I should have, but Hillary warned me that the person she was meeting was Anna's dad. I figured she'd simply made up with him and they were enjoying some time together."

Chase held his pen tighter. "Who is Anna's dad?"

"I don't know. Hillary never told me." Silas's gaze skittered away. "Like I said, our relationship wasn't good for many years."

Chase leaned back in his chair. Silas's story was convoluted, but that didn't make it untrue. And nothing in his statement amounted to a crime. It was time to push him and see where that led. "It's my understanding you were angry with your sister because she received all the inheritance money when your grandparents died. We spoke to some of Hillary's neighbors. They said you threatened her."

A flush rose in Silas's cheeks. He picked at the label on the water bottle with one finger. "I'm not proud of my actions. I was a drunk and a mean one at that. My grandparents were smart to give Hillary the money."

There was no anger in his voice, only embarrassment. Chase tapped his pen against the pad of paper. "Did you kill your sister, Silas?"

His head snapped up. "Absolutely not. I would never hurt Hillary."

"You've been arrested for assault. You've hurt people before. Why not Hillary? She had the money you wanted, the money you deserved. You've got this strange story about dropping her off in town; then she goes missing for hours. You never once try to locate her or call the police—"

Silas slammed a fist on the table. "I didn't kill my sister!"

The passionate flare of anger confirmed Chase's suspicions. Silas had a temper. Had he and Hillary gotten into an argument when she came to see him at the campsite? Or worse, had he lured his sister to the campsite to kill her? It was a possibility that couldn't be taken off the table.

Silas unclenched his fist. He sucked in a deep breath and then let it out slowly. The heat in his cheeks darkened, but the fire went out of his eyes. He sagged against his chair. "I've never hurt anyone while sober. Drunk is a different story. I'll admit that." Silas licked his lips and his leg began jittering again. "I should've reported Hillary missing. In hindsight, I wish I had, but I didn't know she was in trouble."

He met Chase's eyes. "I know this looks bad. I don't have an alibi for the night Hillary died and her truck was in my possession. But you have to believe me, I didn't kill my sister."

Chase studied the man sitting across from him but stayed quiet.

At the moment, he didn't know what to believe.

FOURTEEN

It was late, but Faith was too jittery to sleep.

Moonlight swept into the room through the cracks in the blinds, illuminating her bedroom. She threw the covers to one side and stood. Anna was nestled in the playpen, sleeping soundly. She'd taken a bottle less than forty-five minutes ago and would sleep for another two hours or so, at least. Faith gently swept a hand across the baby's downy hair. The wisps immediately bounced back to their original position, refusing to be tamed. Was that how Anna would be? Wild and fearless? She'd survived more in her young life than anyone should. Already she was tough. She deserved to be cherished and loved. It was a mission Faith was ready to accept.

God, you've brought this child to me. Am I supposed to adopt her? I want to. I have so much love to give.

But was it fair? Faith didn't have a husband. Didn't Anna deserve to have a father who loved her just as much as her mother?

Maybe she already had one. They still didn't know the

identity of Hillary's secret boyfriend. Faith couldn't be sure the man was even aware he had a child. There were a lot of unanswered questions. They swirled in her mind, running rampant despite her best intentions to take things one day at a time. A quick glance at the alarm clock on the nightstand confirmed it was midnight. Maybe some warm milk would ease her mind and body to slumber. Better yet, Marsha's special hot chocolate blend was sitting untouched on the counter.

Faith tucked a blanket around Anna and made sure the baby monitor was on before leaving the bedroom. Her bare feet sank into the carpet. The half-decorated Christmas tree sparkled in the corner of the living room. Light seeped across the floor from the kitchen. Chase sat at the table, laptop open in front of him. He'd changed from his police uniform into a long-sleeved T-shirt and sweatpants. Scamper, her dog, was curled up at his feet.

The sight of Chase in her home was familiar, even in casual clothing, and yet...and yet everything between them felt different now. Every atom in her body was attuned to him in a way Faith had never experienced before. The memory of his kiss was burned into her mind and the echo of that touch imprinted on her lips.

How was she ever going to go back to being just friends with him? What a foolish, foolish woman she was. Their kiss had unlocked a truth buried deep inside her heart. She was in love with Chase. Had been for a lot longer than she wanted to admit to.

And he didn't feel the same way. Or at least...she didn't think he did. But just then, Chase glanced up and caught sight of her. The exhaustion creating deep lines in his forehead eased, and a smile lifted the corners of his lips. He looked at her as if she were the sunshine appearing after a thunderstorm. Fresh hope sprang anew in her heart. The question was on the tip of her tongue, but a sudden wave of fear and nerves trapped the words in her throat. How would she feel if Chase rejected her?

Devastated. And there was still a chance he would. It was better to talk later. There was so much going on with the murder investigation. Until the killer was safely behind bars, the case had to be their focus.

Faith forced a smile. "I couldn't sleep. I thought I'd make some hot chocolate. Do you want any?"

Chase rose from the chair. "I'd love some." He gently snagged her hand and steered her into his empty seat. The wood was still warm from his body. "Sit. I'll make it for us."

She debated arguing with him but decided against it. Scamper rested his head on her leg. She absently stroked his fur and studied the computer screen in front of her. Chase had been making notes about the case. She scanned them. "This is a good summary of the suspects."

He poured milk into a saucepan. "Anything to add?"

Faith read the document more carefully. "I don't know. It's been days since Hillary's murder, but we don't have much to go on." She leaned back in the chair. "Let's take the suspects one by one."

"Fair enough."

"Dr. Whitcomb was in a relationship with Hillary, and their breakup was contentious, but he has an alibi for the night of her murder. Is there any way he could've faked his presence at the hospital? Have you been able to verify the time he arrived and left?"

"Not exactly. The computer system shows he logged in at four for his shift, and the staff verifies he was there, but I don't have a firm timeline of his entire evening. Due to the hectic nature of the ER, doctors and nurses are in and out. It's unlikely Dr. Whitcomb killed Hillary, but it's not impossible." Chase spooned hot chocolate mixture into two cups. "I know you think he looked at Anna strangely—"

"Not to mention the ski mask that fell out of his pocket while we were talking to him."

"Yes, but Dr. Whitcomb drives an SUV, not a silver truck. He wasn't the man who attacked you in the grocery store parking lot or who shot at us while coming home from your parents' house."

Faith frowned and then nodded. Those were valid arguments. She focused back on the list of suspects. "Which brings us to Silas. He had access to Hillary's vehicle, which closely resembles the one used in the attacks against us. No alibi for the night of the murder. And he was in close contact with his sister on the night she disappeared, mere hours before her death."

Faith accepted the steaming mug of hot chocolate from Chase. The comforting scents of vanilla and cinnamon teased her nose. "What do you think about what he said today? About dropping Hillary off in town?"

Chase lowered himself to a kitchen chair and scraped a hand through his hair. "I'm not sure what to think. It's an unlikely story, but that doesn't make it untrue. Officers questioned shops in the center of town, but no one remembers seeing Hillary there. Of course, it's a busy time of year with everyone doing their Christmas shopping."

"So it's possible she was in town but didn't stick out enough for anyone to remember seeing her."

"Exactly." He glowered. "I'm not happy we were forced to release Silas after questioning him. It would make me feel better to know he was behind bars for the night. At the very least, it would give us more time to investigate his story."

Faith shared Chase's sentiment, but Silas hadn't committed a crime. At least, not one that could be proven. The police had no reason to hold him. But Aiden had ordered extra patrols around Faith's property again tonight. It was a kind gesture, and one she appreciated deeply, especially since the police department had limited resources and manpower.

She blew on her hot chocolate and then took a sip. The sweet favors burst across her tongue. She sighed with contentment. Chase drank as well and gave a grunt of surprise. "You weren't lying. This is amazing."

"Isn't it?" She tapped her finger against the warm mug, her thoughts once again turning to the case. If Silas was telling the truth, it left only one other suspect. "What about Tom Bradley? Did you question Hillary's friends again about her relationship with the Bradley family?"

"Yes, and we uncovered something very interesting. According to one of Hillary's friends, she mentioned Tom was flirting with her. Hillary found it uncomfortable and wanted advice on how to handle it. The friend urged her to be direct and then if things didn't stop, to quit."

Faith lowered her mug to the table, the sweet taste of the hot chocolate turning sour in her stomach. "Did she take the friend's advice?"

"Don't know. Hillary never mentioned it again, and her

friend didn't pry. She figured the situation had been resolved."

Faith's mind whirled with the new information. She hated to point fingers at a potentially innocent man, but every avenue had to be investigated. "Tom's advances may have made Hillary uncomfortable initially, but what if things developed between them?"

Her gaze shot to the yard. The barn, with the Christmas wreath on full display, sat illuminated in the lights glowing from the top of the building. Beyond that, the yard was shrouded in darkness.

Faith shuddered. Had she been living next door to a killer all this time? A thought wiggled into her mind, and she gasped. "Chase, Tom owns a car dealership. He has access to all kinds of vehicles, including silver trucks."

"That same thought already occurred to me." Chase drained the last of his hot chocolate. "I've spoken to Aiden, and he's looking into it."

The knot of fear gripping her stomach loosened. She sank against the chair, her gaze once again drifting to the barn. "I can't imagine how terrified Hillary must've been. Even without these attacks on me, her killer needs to be brought to justice."

"He will be." Chase placed a comforting hand over hers.

The warmth of his skin sent a fresh wave of awareness surging through her. Faith's breath hitched, even as her gaze met his. The lighter flecks buried in his cobalt eyes held her focus. Involuntarily, her body leaned closer to him. Chase's gaze dropped to her lips and his own breath seemed shallow.

"Faith…"

The word came out in a husky whisper. Her pulse skittered in response and then skyrocketed as Chase's hand rose to cup her face. His thumb traced a line across the ridge of her cheek before dropping to skim her lips. A blaze of heat followed his touch. Any doubts she had about Chase's feelings evaporated when their gazes met once more. Love, pure and simple, shone in the depths of his eyes. But something else lingered there too.

Fear. Worry. It hit her all at once that Faith wasn't the only one struggling to make sense of the recent developments between them. She reached up to clasp his hand in hers. They needed to talk, and if he didn't stop touching her, she was going to give in to her desire and kiss him instead. "Chase, there's something I need to say. I'm in love with you. I've been too scared to tell you for so many reasons, but I don't want to be afraid anymore. The timing is terrible, I know, but…"

He blinked, as if dazed by her statement. Faith's chest squeezed tight. "Chase?"

A slow smile lifted the corners of his handsome mouth. He rose and gently tugged her into a standing position before wrapping his arms around her waist. Chase lowered his mouth to hers. The kiss was tender and sweet. Filled with promise. Over far too quickly.

When he pulled back, Chase met her gaze. "I've been waiting years to hear those words."

Shock vibrated through her. "Years? But you never said…I didn't know…"

He brushed his mouth against hers. "I didn't want you to know. For a long time, I wasn't sure marriage or a family was for me. The relationship with my dad messed me up. I never felt worthy of you."

"You've always been good enough for me." She cupped his face in her hands and the bristles of his beard scratched against her palm. "Your father's mistakes have nothing to do with you."

"I know that now. And spending time with you and Anna only cemented what my heart already knew. I want a family. More importantly, I want you. You're my best friend, Faith, and the only woman I ever want to spend my life with. I love you."

Her heart soared. The love shining in his eyes warmed her straight through. She wanted to stay in his arms and never leave. "Chase—"

Gunshots interrupted her.

FIFTEEN

Chase's muscles tightened. The gunshots had come from outside, near the front of the house. He bolted across the living room to the windows overlooking the driveway. Red and blue lights strobed across the grass. The driver's side door to the patrol car was open, but David wasn't visible. Had his fellow officer shot at an intruder? Or worse, had he been shot?

Within moments, Chase had palmed his gun and his cell phone. He called the attack into dispatch while hustling Faith down the hallway toward her bedroom and the baby. His best friend needed no urging. She raced to collect Anna from the playpen. The baby was still sleeping as she settled into the crook of Faith's arms.

He loved them. Both of them. Chase was going to marry Faith. His future was with her and, God willing, with Anna too. The fear of losing them forever if the killer succeeded in his mission was nearly crippling in its intensity.

Chase had to make sure that didn't happen. He wouldn't *allow* it to happen.

"Come on." He lightly took Faith's arm and tugged her down the hallway, back toward the kitchen. The bedroom only had windows. If the killer made it inside the house, they had limited means of escape. Chase had planned for every contingency. He needed to get them to a place where they had access to both the front and back doors. Backup was on the way, but it would take time for them to reach the house. How long he wasn't certain. He'd hung up on dispatch to call David. The officer wasn't answering.

That fueled the worry coursing through Chase's veins. He shot off a text message to his friend but didn't get a response. Chase didn't want to consider what that could mean. David was a good friend, and the urge to race outside to his aid was a strong one, but Chase couldn't leave Faith and Anna unprotected. He sent up a silent prayer for David's safety.

Chase paused in the hallway, listening for any noise that didn't belong. The quick tick of the grandfather clock melded with the sound of his own heartbeat and Faith's quick breathing.

Nothing. The intruder hadn't entered the house. Not yet.

The living room was centered in the house and provided the most visibility. He guided Faith near the Christmas tree and urged her to crouch low. The bar separating the kitchen from the rest of the house would provide cover if the killer shot through any of the windows. The twinkling lights on the tree played against her hair and illuminated the fearful look in her eyes. Somewhere along the way, she'd grabbed a knife. She clutched the weapon in one hand while keeping the baby safe in the other. Scamper, sensing the danger to his mistress, took a protective stance next to her.

"Stay here," Chase whispered.

Faith nodded sharply. He squeezed her hand in a comforting gesture before releasing it and taking several steps toward the windows overlooking the front yard. His vision blurred, and he stumbled. Chase's hand shot out. He grabbed the back of the armchair and steadied himself. He blinked rapidly to clear his vision. The room spun.

What on earth?

He'd been in dangerous situations before—life-threatening ones, even—but he'd never experienced anything like this. Chase shook off the sudden wave of dizziness and forced himself to take a few more steps. Time seemed to move in slow motion. Something slammed into his knees and it took Chase far too long to realize he'd fallen to the carpet. A heartbeat later and Faith was by his side. His vision swam again and he could sense she was talking to him, but her voice sounded very far away, as though she was in a tunnel.

His muscles went slack and he slid the rest of the way to the carpet. Someplace, in the back of his foggy mind, his brain registered what'd happened.

Drugged. He'd been drugged.

In the hot chocolate?

He tried to move his mouth, to warn Faith, but the words wouldn't come.

The world went black.

"Chase!" Faith shook his shoulder, panic welling in her chest as his eyes rolled back in his head and he became unresponsive. Had he been shot? She hadn't heard a bullet, nor was there any blood, but something was terribly wrong. She pressed her fingers to his neck and found a strong and steady pulse. His breathing was also regular.

Faith's head swam as a sudden wave of dizziness overcame her. Anna, still nestled in the crook of her left arm, was so heavy. A wet tongue scraped across Faith's cheek, snapping her mind into focus. Scamper. The dog was next to her. He nudged her shoulder and Faith belatedly realized she must've closed her eyes for a moment. They were so heavy.

Unnaturally heavy. She'd been drugged. It was the only thing that made sense. And the only thing she'd had in the last half an hour was the hot chocolate. Chase had finished his entire mug, but Faith only had about half. Whatever had been in the mix wasn't strong enough to render her unconscious. At least, not yet.

Scamper growled, the sound low and deep in his chest. It sent Faith's heart into overdrive. She shook Chase's shoulder once more, calling his name, but he remained unresponsive. Giving up, she palmed the sharp knife she'd taken from the kitchen. Chase's gun rested on the floor next to him, but Faith didn't know how to shoot. She wouldn't even be able to figure out how to get the safety off.

Heart pounding, she followed Scamper's gaze to the front door. The handle twisted, first one way, then the other. A scream lodged itself in Faith's throat. She clutched Anna closer to her chest. The baby was still sleeping, thankfully, long lashes resting against her chubby cheeks.

No one was going to hurt this child. No one.

God, give me strength.

She would need it. How could she protect Anna and defend an unconscious Chase with nothing more than a knife? Her gaze frantically bounced around the room, seeking answers. The flashing bulbs on the Christmas tree drew her attention. The cheery lights were a sharp contrast to the fear coursing through her veins, but then a flash of inspiration struck her.

Faith scurried across the living room. Several presents rested under the Christmas tree branches. One box was large. She tossed the top off and quickly removed the cozy blanket inside. It was a gift for her mother, who loved curling up on the couch at night with a cup of tea to watch her shows. Ever so gently, Faith laid a still sleeping Anna into the empty box. "Stay quiet, little one."

The baby sighed, completely unaware of the danger coming their way. Faith replaced the lid on the box, careful to leave a corner elevated for fresh air. Then she patted Scamper's head. "Guard, boy."

She gathered the blanket just as movement shifted on the porch. A dark shadow, large enough to be a man, appeared in the window pane. Seconds later, glass shattered, and a hand reached in to unlock the door. Bile rose in Faith's throat. She clutched the blanket to her chest, as if it was a baby, and shot to her full height. Her mind raced. Would her trick work? In the dark, and at a glance, she prayed the attacker would believe she had Anna wrapped up in her blanket.

The door burst open. For one heart stopping moment,

Faith was face-to-face with the masked man. Light glinted off the gun in his hand.

She screamed. Spinning on her heel, Faith bolted for the kitchen. Scamper barked furiously. She prayed it was enough to prevent the intruder from going anywhere near the old dog. And subsequently, Anna's hiding place. Footsteps pounded behind her as the gunman gave chase. Her fingers fumbled with the lock and then frigid air washed over her heated cheeks as she stumbled into the night.

The grass was icy under her soles. A bullet whizzed past, close enough to ruffle Faith's hair. Another scream lodged in her throat. She kept moving, drawing the killer farther from the house and away from everything she loved dearly. It was a reckless and dangerous move. One Chase would never approve of, but Faith couldn't think of another way to save him and Anna.

Another gunshot rang out. Survival instinct took over as Faith bolted across the lawn for the barn. Her breath came in gasps as she darted around the structure. The mud threatened to upend her. For one brief terrifying moment, Faith imagined herself as Hillary. Clutching her child, blindly running, terror fueling her movements. The woods were dark shadows in the distance. If she could lure the gunman into them, then it might buy enough time for the police to arrive. She gripped the knife and added more fuel to her steps.

A shape loomed large and Faith stumbled back. She landed hard on her rear. Pain shot through her back and the blanket tumbled from her arms. The attacker snatched it and gave a growl of frustration when he realized it was empty.

CHRISTMAS THREAT

Faith scrambled to get her feet, but wasn't fast enough. The attacker snagged her arm with a gloved hand. He jabbed the gun into her side. The cold metal of the barrel pressed into her skin.

Faith froze.

"Where is she?" he snarled. Then he shook her violently, his voice rising. "Where is she?"

"Gone!" she yelled the word. Even through the haze of her fear, the attacker's voice was familiar. It was Tom, her neighbor. Faith couldn't allow him to get his hands on Anna. "She's gone. The social worker took her to a family in the next county to keep her safe."

The lie spilled from her lips in a shaky voice. She forced herself to meet the gaze of the man trying to kill her. His eyes were black pits of evil, visible through the slits in the ski mask, and a river of icy fear ran down her spine.

His breathing was ragged. Then Tom's grip on her arm tightened, and he slammed her against a pine tree. Pain ricocheted through her brain as her skull collided with the rough wood. The gun dug harder into her side.

"Don't lie to me. I know you've hidden her somewhere, probably in the house." He twisted her around and began dragging her in that direction.

"You won't get away with this, Tom. The police are already on the way."

If he was surprised she'd discovered his identity, it didn't show. He ignored her comment and kept moving. Faith held tight to the knife, but the angle was all wrong. She couldn't disarm him. She also couldn't allow him to get back inside the house. He'd kill them all.

Faith dug her heels into the grass, hoping to slow their

progress across the yard. "What are you going to do to Anna? You can't hurt her. She's just a baby."

This time, her words garnered a reaction. Tom's iron hold on her arm tightened even more. "That...*thing* has caused me more grief than I care to admit. She's not a baby to me. She's eighteen years worth of child support that I'm not interested in paying."

His tone was harsh and cold. Faith dropped her body weight, making it harder for Tom to drag her. "You killed Hillary. The two of you had an affair, but when she got pregnant with Anna, you didn't want to have anything to do with her. That's why she moved to Austin. But she came back. She saw her brother and then she brought Anna to meet you." Faith didn't actually expect him to respond. She kept talking, putting the facts they'd gather during the investigation together. "You drove them to your house. Your wife was on vacation, visiting her family."

Faith remembered that tidbit from their first conversation at her house. Tom had tried to push the investigation toward Dr. Whitcomb. He'd done a good job acting upset over Hillary's death. "The next morning, you had an argument with Hillary. She wanted you to be a father to her baby, to pay child support."

Whatever happened had scared Hillary. She took Anna and bolted from Tom's house. Ran through the woods searching for safety, ending up in Faith's yard. Tom killed her in the barn, carried her back to his house, and then went back for the baby. But Faith had already found Anna.

Tom had been trying to cover up his affair and the subsequent murder ever since. That's why he needed to get rid of Anna. A DNA test would prove he was the father.

They were halfway across the yard now. Faith struggled to slow their progress even more. She strained to listen for any sound of the police. Where were they? She twisted the knife around in her fingers, tightening her grip on the only weapon she had left. "You drugged the hot chocolate. How did you know we'd drink it? Or when?"

"There's a listening device in the basket. I couldn't take any more chances." Tom glared at her. "You and Hillary. You've caused me a bunch of unnecessary trouble."

Faint sirens wailed in the distance. It was now or never. Faith twisted her body and jabbed the knife into Tom's arm.

He screamed. The hand holding her loosened, and Faith wasted no time. She whirled, racing for the barn door. She shoved it open and bolted inside. Poppy pawed at the ground in her stall. The scent of hay and horse hung heavy in the air.

Faith's heart thundered in her chest as her feet pounded against the concrete floor. The police officers would come to the front of the house. She needed to get there, and the fastest way was through the barn.

Her gaze narrowed to the door on the other side. Behind her came the sound of angry footsteps. Tom wasn't giving up.

The barn door swung open, frigid air rushing in as a large shadow filled the doorway. Chase. His hand shot out, and he shoved Faith to the ground, raising his weapon. Shots erupted in the space. Faith's eyes squeezed shut, prayers on her lips.

Moments later, she was gathered in Chase's arms. She gripped his shirt with one hand, sobs rising in her chest as she clung to him. He was solid and whole. Alive. Faith kept her eyes closed, unwilling to look at the other side of the barn. "Is he...is he...?"

Chase's lips caressed her temple. "It's over, sweetheart. It's all over."

SIXTEEN

One year later

Chase gently clasped Anna's two chubby hands. She took one step, then another. Her velvet dress and matching bow brought out the color in her cheeks, but her feet were bare. She gripped the carpet with her toes. On the floor, next to the Christmas tree, Faith clapped and held out her hands. The diamond engagement ring next to her wedding band sparkled. "Come to mommy, sweet girl. Come on."

Anna laughed and smiled. She wobbled, but her grip on Chase's fingers helped the fourteen-month-old regain her balance. Once he knew she was steady on her feet, Chase eased his fingers from hers. He quickly took out his phone and started recording. Scamper opened one eye from his bed in the corner of the room, assessed the situation, and went back to sleep. A baby's first steps weren't very interesting. The steak he'd gulped down earlier, however, had been worth getting up for.

"Anna, come on. You can do it." Faith waved the baby forward. Her dark hair was swept away from her face and her eyes shone with excitement. "Come to mommy."

Mommy. Daddy. How much their lives had changed in a year. Faith and Chase had gotten married just a few weeks after the attack last Christmas. They'd immediately petitioned to adopt Anna. The formal paperwork had been signed last week. Anna was officially their daughter and would always be.

Hillary's photograph was on their mantel alongside other family shots. She deserved the place of honor. She'd fought with her very last breath to protect her child. When Anna was older, they would tell her the truth about her birth mother. Sadly, they would also have to tell her about Tom. But Chase had firsthand experience in what it was like to have a parent who made terrible decisions. He would make sure Anna knew that her biological father's choices had nothing to do with her.

She was a child of God. She was loved.

Anna's sweet brow crinkled as she concentrated on Faith. For a moment, Chase was certain Anna would sit down, as she had so many times before. But then her little foot slid forward. His breath hitched.

Faith waved her hands. "That's it, little one. Come on."

Anna lifted her other foot and took a step. Then another. She tumbled into her mother's waiting hands and Faith showered her face with kisses. "You did it! Chase, did you see that? She did it."

"I absolutely saw it." He waved his phone in the air. "Got it on video too." He dropped down next to his girls. Anna giggled and crawled into his lap. Chase's heart constricted when she laid her head on his chest. He kissed the top of her sweet head. "I think someone needs a nap."

"It's about that time." Faith smiled. "We wanted to give you a present first."

She reached under the tree and pulled out a small package. Chase took it from her, confused. "But it's only Christmas Eve. Why don't you save it for tomorrow?"

"The whole family will be here in a few hours to celebrate the holiday with us. I wanted to give you this present while it was just the three of us." Faith leaned over and kissed him softly on the lips. Then her smile widened. "Open it."

Chase lifted the lid from the box. Nestled among a cloud of cotton was a pregnancy test. A positive pregnancy test. His heart skittered as his gaze lifted to meet his wife's. "Is this..? Are you...?"

He couldn't form a full sentence. Tears filled Faith's eyes and her hands went to her waist. "We're having a baby."

"That's the best Christmas present I've ever received." Chase's throat closed, and he had to blink back his own tears of happiness. He pulled Faith close and kissed her. Then he wrapped his arm around her shoulders. Anna was still nestled against his chest. His family. His life.

"Thank you, Faith." His mouth brushed against her hair. "For everything. You've made me a very happy man."

She snuggled into his embrace with a contented sigh. "I love you, Chase."

"I love you too."

ALSO BY LYNN SHANNON

Texas Ranger Heroes Series

Ranger Protection

Ranger Redemption

Ranger Courage

Ranger Faith

Ranger Honor

Triumph Over Adversity Series

Calculated Risk

Critical Error

Necessary Peril

Would you like to know when my next book is released? Or when my novels go on sale? It's easy. Subscribe to my newsletter at www.lynnshannon.com and all of the info will come straight to your inbox!

Reviews help readers find books. Please consider leaving a review at your favorite place of purchase or anywhere you discover new books. Thank you.

Made in the USA
Monee, IL
03 July 2022